THE CABIN AT SILVER LAKE

A MYSTERY THRILLER

MICHELLE FILES

Edited by
CECILY BROOKES

MICHELLEFILES.COM

INTRODUCTION

Two couples. A cold night in a cabin deep in the forest.

Having a great time with their friends, two couples are drinking wine and laughing. It all turns on a dime when they realize they are not alone. The night turns into a nightmare.

But that's not the worst part.

The fallout has friend turning on friend. Husband turning on wife. And everyone is lying to the sheriff.

The investigation leads to an unlikely suspect.

Read to the exciting conclusion. Can you figure out what really happened that fateful night in the cabin?

A rollercoaster of a thriller from start to finish.

Coming Soon:

Book 2 in the Silver Lake Mystery Series -

The Disappearance of Zoe Carter

CHAPTER 1

SIX MONTHS AGO

"Make sure you take the sledgehammers with you." The man pointed at the two thugs sitting across the cafe table from him. He glanced around at the nearby tables and leaned in, his face only inches from the men in front of him. "You, Dante, don't forget to bring zip ties and duffle bags. That's your one job. Think you can handle it?"

Leaning back in his chair, Dante shrugged and ran his pudgy fingers through the scruffy brown hair that hadn't seen the inside of a shower in at least a week. "Yeah, Boss, I think I can handle that," a touch of sarcasm leaking through.

"Yeah, maybe you can, maybe you can't. But after what happened last time…"

Dante's hand shot up, interrupting what the man was about to say. "That wasn't my fault and you know it. That was all on Angelo here." He gave a quick sideways head tilt toward the man sitting on his left.

Angelo flew out of his seat. "Bullshit! You know damn well that..."

The coffee shop was busier than they would have liked. It was a Monday after lunch, not a time when anyone expected a crowd. But they were already there and needed to sort out their plan. It was a place none of them were familiar with, since they wanted to meet far from where they would be using those sledgehammers.

The pale green walls and eclectic decorating style gave the place a cozy feeling. One wall was lined with bookshelves filled to the brim with old, worn paperbacks. They were free for the taking. Most people who took one, also brought one from home to replace it, or returned the book to the shelves after reading it. It was a favorite hangout of the locals, and had been a town staple for close to fifty years.

The man looked around at the patrons. Most appeared to be over forty years old and were sipping a cup of coffee or tea. He was unsure as to why it was an older crowd, but being a Monday afternoon probably had something to do with that. Not a single twenty-something in sight.

Some of the customers had a muffin or croissant, or even a fruit cup sitting on the table, half eaten, next to them. Almost every single person was either immersed in a book or typing away furiously on their keyboards. He was not a technical person himself, and could never understand the fascination people had with perusing the internet. There was so much more out in the world that didn't involve sitting and staring at a computer all day.

Two elderly women, seventy-five at least, were sitting at the table next to his trio of men. One of the women had a cane leaning against her chair. Her buttoned blouse was stretched to the brim. That could be dangerous for her friend, sitting across from her. One loose button, and an emergency trip to the eye doctor would be in order.

Her friend was wearing a sweatsuit, was thinner, and looked to be much more athletic. How such two seemingly different people came to be friends, was anyone's guess.

The women had no phones or computers on the table in front of them. Only teacups and muffins. They spoke in hushed tones, and smiles, and seemed to be thoroughly enjoying their time together. An occasional glance over from the women when one of the men was a bit too loud for the subdued location, was not completely unexpected.

The man gave a quick nod and smiled at the women. On one hand, he wondered how boring it must be for them to be doing nothing but talking to each other. On the other hand, he was a bit envious at how easy their conversation seemed. There was no doubt in his mind that they had known each other for many many years, probably a lifetime.

Sitting in a coffee shop was not his idea of a good time. He much preferred working on his car, or taking his wife out for a drive or a movie. He loved being out and about in the world. His wife was the same. They made the perfect pair.

Angelo's outburst caused patrons of the cafe to watch them with eyebrows raised and a hint of a smile on their faces. They were clearly enjoying the show. One man hung up his phone as he stared at them. Clearly their table was much more interesting than whoever it was that he was talking with.

This lasted only a moment though, before the curious faces turned back to their electronic devices.

"Okay, okay, you two, people are starting to stare. Angelo, sit down. The last thing we need is for people to notice us. And most of all, remember us. People remembering us could be our downfall. We need to keep as incognito as possible. Got it?"

Both men nodded and Angelo sat back down, glaring at Dante as he did so. "Yeah, yeah, we got it."

CHAPTER 2

Angelo was a fairly large man. At six feet, four inches tall, most men looked up to him. He had just turned thirty years old and with his shortly cropped black hair and bright green eyes, he was popular with the ladies. But he was single and wanted to keep it that way.

Being with one woman for the rest of his life made his skin crawl. He treated the women he dated well, but that was it. No promises, no long-term anything. They knew this from the beginning.

Of course, that motto didn't always work out the way he wanted it to. Occasionally, someone he dated got a bit too clingy and he had to set them straight. He hated to see a woman cry, but it came with the territory.

Women are monogamous by nature. He just wasn't. It had never even crossed his mind to stay with only one woman. He always wondered what the point of that was.

Then there was that one time that Monique, the relationship from hell, as he liked to call it, decided to stalk him when he ended things with her. It took a good eight months of nightly phone calls and knocks on the door, along with

Angelo threatening to end her, before she finally gave up and found someone else to focus her attention on.

Those were some tense months for Angelo, and it did teach him to be a bit more direct with women. He thought he had always been direct, but clearly not quite enough. He needed to make sure that they understood that his decision was final and there was no hope for a reconciliation. He was never sure if his new tactic worked or not, but he never had another issue with a woman who just wouldn't go away.

Dante, on the other hand, was only five feet, seven inches tall. He had a stocky build and gruff exterior. He was the same age as Angelo. Due to an unfortunate bicycle accident as a teenager, his nose was permanently crooked. Though he had a steady girlfriend, the ladies never clamored for his attention.

Angelo and Dante were cousins. They had grown up on the same rough street their entire childhood. Some petty thefts and minor burglaries peppered their juvenile records. Both sets of parents had drug problems, and had pretty much given up on dealing with the boys and their problems. Their parents had their own issues to overcome.

By the time the pair were in their late-twenties, both of them had spent the majority of their adult lives in prison. Drugs and robberies were their own life choices and they were paying for them.

Prison is where they met the 'Boss.' He was only a few years older than them, but was someone who people took notice of, and listened to. He just had that way about him, and people were naturally drawn to him.

Once all three were paroled, they began working together. Burglarizing empty homes while people were out of town became their primary source of income. They didn't fear security cameras, or even alarm systems. Prison taught them a lot of things, namely how to get past an alarm system. Ski masks took care of the cameras.

They had devised a routine that had them in the house, straight to the primary bedroom, tear it apart looking for jewelry and cash, and out of the house in under five minutes. Even if the alarm went off, it didn't worry them much. By the time the alarm company called and spoke with the owners, and then decided to call the police, it would still be a few minutes before they arrived. They were always long gone by then.

Even as teenagers, the boys found out that most people kept their valuables in their bedrooms, which is why they made a beeline for that room.

Sure, some of them thought they were clever, hiding their valuables in their dressers, on their bookshelves, and even in their medicine cabinets. They had seen it all. The two of them even went through pockets of clothes hanging in the closets. People were not as clever as they liked to think they were.

During all of this, the Boss never accompanied them inside the houses. It was his job to scope them out and watch the family's habits. He would learn when people were leaving, and when they would be returning. He would then watch for anyone coming home during the burglary, just in case. He was never the getaway car. The Boss wanted to keep separate from what Angelo and Dante were doing, in case everything fell apart. He always drove his own car, parked on the next block over, and walked over, keeping hidden during the burglary.

Angelo and Dante had to bring their own transportation, which they would park several houses down. So far, it had all worked out perfectly. There was only one close call. The teenage neighbor of a family gone on a Caribbean vacation was scheduled to come every couple of days to check on the family cat. She had been tasked with feeding and scooping.

The Boss was not aware of the cat. The teenager had decided that she would spend that particular night at the house, along with her boyfriend. When Angelo and Dante entered the owners' bedroom they were in for a big surprise. It was 2:25 a.m. and the two teens were fast asleep.

The girl, having been startled awake by the intruders, began screaming. Her boyfriend leaped out of the bed, stark naked, and ran at them. The whole thing would have been comical if it weren't for the fact that Dante had a gun in his pocket.

Before the boy could get within five feet of them, Dante fired, killing him instantly. The poor girl met the same fate, after Dante had a bit of fun with her. Angelo wanted nothing to do with any of that. He grabbed the jewelry box off the dresser and left Dante stranded.

The two of them had been at odds ever since.

CHAPTER 3

The snow outside the windows of the cafe that dark Monday afternoon gave the entire place an even more cozy feeling. An array of colorful coats and hats hung on the wooden stand by the front door and a swift chill made those closest to the door shiver every time it was opened.

The smell of fresh snow always made Angelo smile. It was one if his favorite things about the late autumn. It was an unusually early snow this year, but welcomed by all, after the humid summer they had just endured. Angelo had called it "A devil's armpit of a summer."

"Listen," the man continued, watching the patrons in the coffee shop out of the side of his eye. Many of them averted their gaze once they realized that he had caught them staring.

One woman, mid-fifties, he surmised, didn't seem to care that he saw her watching them. She continued, defiantly watching them over the rim of her coffee cup. Setting it down in front of her, she locked eyes with the Boss. He watched her for another minute before turning his attention back to his own table.

Why he had chosen a public place such as this to meet, he didn't know. Next time...if there was a next time...they would meet somewhere remote and quiet.

"Tomorrow night, show up around eight. Go in the back door once you see that the women are alone, probably in the kitchen yapping. Get the women first. Don't hurt them." He met Dante's gaze. "I'm talking to you." Dante looked down at the table. "Once they are subdued, then you can finish your task. You know what to do. Get in, get out. Don't muck around. Any questions?"

"Yeah," Dante asked. "How do you know where it is? Or even if it's there at all? What if we don't find anything?"

"Because I have contacts, dumbass. No one else has the balls to go after it, like I do," the Boss declared.

He glanced back over at the middle-aged woman, who was still watching them with interest. She had put a bookmark in the book she had been reading and it was sitting on the table in front of her. It seemed as if there was nothing more interesting going on in the whole world at that moment, other than what the three interesting men were talking about. He narrowed his eyes at her. She didn't flinch.

Turning back once again to the men in front of him, what the Boss didn't say was that the 'contacts' who gave him information were thugs and thieves. Rumors had a way of getting out of control. He didn't even know for sure if they would find what they were looking for. But he was damn sure willing to find out.

"When are we getting paid?" Dante blurted out.

The man's eyes narrowed and he once again leaned in, shifting his eyes around the room. "Are you a complete idiot? Keep your voice down. Have I ever not paid you?"

Dante shrugged. "No. But I got rent to pay."

"Then shut the hell up. I told you that we will meet up Saturday. That hasn't changed."

"But what if…"

"There is no *what if*, Dante. I'll see you Saturday, get you paid, and that'll be that."

The boss stood and walked over to the woman sitting alone at the table watching them. Angelo and Dante stayed where they were, wondering what was about to happen. He sat in the chair next to her and scooted it as close as he could get. Her eyes went wide.

He leaned in and spoke in just barely more than a whisper. "Lady, I don't know what your problem is, or if you are just an incredibly nosey bitch, but I suggest that you pick up your book there," he tipped his head in that direction, "and leave this place immediately. Otherwise I'll have to start thinking you are a threat to us. I don't like threats. Comprende?"

He pulled back to look at her face. She nodded quickly, grabbed her book, and couldn't get out of the coffee shop fast enough. Angelo and Dante watched the encounter with interest.

Walking back over to his table, he remained standing. He turned to Angelo. "How about you? Anything you don't understand?"

"Naw Boss, we're all good," Angelo replied.

CHAPTER 4

The air was crisp that early fall morning in the woods surrounding Silver Lake.

Most of the trees were evergreen pines and cedars. But interspersed among them, golden aspens shimmered in the morning sunlight, their delicate, heart-shaped leaves trembling in a soft breeze. The vibrant contrast of their yellow hues against the dark pines was striking.

Here and there, clusters of maples blazed with fiery orange and red leaves, their vibrant colors signaling the arrival of early fall. The forest floor was a tapestry of fallen leaves, pine needles, and patches of moss, giving off a fresh, earthy aroma.

The air was cool and crisp, carrying hints of resin from the pines and the subtle sweetness of decaying leaves. Gentle rustling from the trees combined with the occasional scuffle of a critter nearby or the chatter of a squirrel, adding life to this peaceful scene.

Rosie and Elena strolled along the well worn winding forest path, their steps light, yet purposeful, as they embraced the crispness of the early morning. The couple inches of snow on the ground did not deter their morning walking ritual.

The women's voices blended harmoniously with the gentle rustle of leaves and the occasional chirp of waking birds. As they walked, Rosie animatedly recounted a story, her hands punctuating the air, while Elena laughed, her cheeks rosy from both the crisp air and their steady pace. The faint scent of pine and earth surrounded them, energizing their conversation and their exercise, as they found balance in the serenity of the moment.

"So you and Sergio are still coming over tonight for dinner and drinks, right?" Rosie asked Elena.

"Yeah of course. I can't wait to see your new cabin now that you are all moved in. I'm so excited that you two live nearby now," Elena told her.

A squawk overhead caused both women to slow down and look up.

"What the heck was that?" Rosie asked.

Elena shrugged. "Probably just a crow. They are kind of obnoxious."

"Yeah, I guess so. That thing was really loud." Her eyes crinkled in the corners as she laughed.

"You'll get used to it," Elena told her. "They are everywhere around here."

"You guys want to come over around six?" Rosie asked, changing the subject.

"Perfect. We'll bring a couple bottles of wine."

"Now that you two live in Silver Lake, we can see each other all the time," Elena told her.

The town of Silver Lake sat high up in the California mountains. Once upon a time, those who flocked to the area were not there for skiing. They came for the gold. Many old gold mines peppered the mountains. By now, most of the mines had caved in, been filled in, or gated, to protect thrill seekers and adventurers from themselves.

Why it was named Silver Lake, instead of Gold Lake, was anybody's guess.

Once those mines were shut down, folks in the area learned to do without. The mountain was full of people in their tiny cabins just trying to survive. No one who wasn't a resident ventured up the steep, winding roads, unless they had to.

Over time, a town grew around the lake. With that, the ski area opened, and the tourists came.

The picturesque town, surrounding the banks of the lake is now the center of everything that happened on the mountain. The shopping area is lovingly called the "Village" by the locals.

"Oh hey, we saw a restaurant in town the other day called Blues," Rosie said. "We might go there for breakfast soon. Have you been there?"

Elena smiled at the mention of Blues Restaurant. It was owned by a couple of her friends, whose family opened it over fifty years ago. Blues was a staple in town and the sort of place where everyone just kind of hung out with friends when nothing else was going on. In a town the size of Silver Lake, that was quite often.

"Yeah, you should definitely check it out," Elena told her. "It's kind of the unofficial hangout for the locals. The owners, Donovan and Savannah, are good friends of mine."

"Well why don't you and Sergio come have breakfast there with us next week? It'll be fun. You can introduce us to your friends," Rosie added. "It would be nice to get to know more people around here."

The women came upon the edge of the forest and the beauty of the lake opened up in front of them.

"Wow. I don't think I'll ever tire of that view," Rosie said. "It's just breathtaking."

"Yeah, it really is. And now that you live here, you can see it every day. It never gets old."

Over the next half hour, the friends strolled along the dirt path that wrapped around the lake.

"I need to get back," Rosie announced. "Tommy is expecting me to help finish unpacking. There are still some things that need to be done before you come over tonight."

A few minutes later they arrived back at their cars parked at the trailhead.

"See you tonight." Rosie waved back over her shoulder as she climbed into her car and drove toward their new cabin.

Living in Silver Lake had been a dream of Rosie's for years. The big city was just too much for her. She had longed for a simpler life. A life in the mountains, in a small town, where everyone knew everyone, sounded just wonderful to her. She dreamed of walking along the city's main street and stopping to talk with friends along the way. That was something that never happened in the big city, where she had to drive everywhere.

She smiled at the fact that they had finally seized the opportunity to work from home. Rosie and Tommy owned an accounting firm. It was something they could do from home, but had never done so, instead keeping their office downtown. Since deciding to move to the mountains, they closed their office, and downsized their staff. Now, just the two of them took care of the customers, along with one employee, who helped with the phones and scheduling. It was the perfect situation for them.

Rosie couldn't have been any happier.

CHAPTER 5

Rosie Allen drove home from her walk with Elena, smiling the entire way. It took them so long to get to Silver Lake full time, that it felt like it would never actually happen. But now that they were here, she couldn't be any happier about it.

As Rosie navigated the winding mountain road toward her secluded cabin, the headlights of her old Jeep cut through the dense fog rolling in from the valley. The familiar scent of pine and damp earth filled the crisp morning air, but a shiver ran down her spine as she spotted a car idling on the side of the road up ahead—its dark shape barely visible in the mist.

It was an old sedan, unmarked and unfamiliar, its engine humming low. The driver, a dark figure that she couldn't see clearly behind the wheel, appeared to be watching her. Rosie couldn't shake the feeling of unseen eyes following her. Clutching the steering wheel tighter, she pressed the gas, eager to put distance between herself and the eerie presence, her pulse quickening with every turn that brought her closer to home.

Heart pounding, Rosie pulled into her driveway, gravel crunching beneath her tires as she threw the car into park.

The image of the man she had passed on the road—his hunched frame, the way he had turned to watch her with hollow, shadowed eyes—clung to her mind like a bad dream.

Stepping out, she darted to the front door, fumbling with her keys before finally shoving it open and slamming it shut behind her. She twisted the deadbolt, then checked it twice before rushing to the back door and locking that too. Every window was latched, every curtain drawn. Standing in the dim glow of her living room lamp light, she listened, straining for the sound of footsteps on the gravel outside. Nothing. Just the wind in the trees. But the uneasy feeling remained, curling in her stomach like a warning.

After a quick search, she found Tommy in the loft working on his computer. He wanted to get the books done for their largest accounting client, before the weekend. He was so engrossed in his work, that he hadn't even noticed she was back home.

"Hey."

Tommy jumped and turned to see his wife standing at the top of the stairs. "What the hell? You scared the life outta me. Did you ninja your way up the stairs? I didn't hear a thing."

Rosie smiled. "Yeah, I'm a ninja. Or maybe I have wings and just floated up, like an angel." She lost her smile. "Seriously, don't be so jumpy."

He kept one eye on the computer screen as they spoke. "So, what's up?" barely registering what she had said. "I want to get this done before Sergio and Elena get here."

"Nothing's up. Oh well...something might be up. When I was driving up the road to our house just now, there was some guy sitting in his car, watching me."

That got his attention, and he released the mouse he had been holding, finally turning his full body toward his wife. "What do you mean, *watching you?*"

"He was just sitting there, watching me. That's it, nothing else."

"Ok honey, I'm gonna need more information than that. Did he roll his window down? Did he get out of his car? Did he follow you to the house?"

Tommy stood and walked over to the window, peering out toward the road. It was at least a quarter mile to the main road. He couldn't see a thing beyond the thick canopy of trees.

"Well?"

"Well what?" she replied, hands on her hips. "I told you that he didn't do anything. He just sat there and watched me drive by."

"And he didn't do anything else?"

Rosie shook her head. "I told you no."

"Hmm, maybe I should go out and see what he wants."

"No, don't do that. What if he's dangerous?" she asked.

"What if he was just lost and trying to get a gps signal?" Tommy asked right back. "Either way, I would like to know. We are kind of sitting ducks out here, if someone wants to mess with us."

"Why would he mess with us?" she asked. "We don't have anything. Not really anyway. This cabin isn't even that big and my car is what, twelve years old? I don't think we are prime targets."

"Probably not," he replied. "But I'm going to go find out."

Rosie let out an exasperated breath. "Fine. Do what you want. But don't come crying to me when he murders you in the forest."

Tommy closed the gap between them in two large steps, wrapping one strong arm around her waist and the other cupping the back of her head. Rosie squealed. He leaned in and kissed her deeply, and she just melted into it.

God he loved this woman.

Five minutes later, Tommy was pulling out of the driveway in the old Jeep. They had another, newer car, but both of them loved the Jeep so much, they drove it most of the time.

In his absence, Rosie began cleaning the cabin. They always kept it tidy, but it needed a good dusting, sweeping, and wiping down.

She and Tommy had met in high school, almost twenty years prior. They ran in separate circles. Tommy was on the football team, and was quite popular. Especially with the girls. He and Rosie ran into each other one day, quite literally, as he was jogging backward in the hallway in an attempt to catch a football his friend had thrown, when he bowled her over.

Her books and homework scattered. In her usual sassiness, Rosie told him to get down on the floor and pick up every last piece of paper for her. She stood over him as he did so. She was not the one who was embarrassed. Tommy had the bright red face, but he did as he was told.

Once finished, he straightened each item into a nice little stack and handed them to her sheepishly.

She smiled at him. "Thank you," and turned to get to her next class.

Tommy, football completely forgotten, jogged to catch up. "What's your name?"

They had been together ever since.

CHAPTER 6

Rosie stood by the window, her arms crossed tightly over her chest as she watched her husband, Tommy, walk toward their car.

Her stomach twisted with unease, her mind racing through worst-case scenarios. What if this person was dangerous? What if they had a weapon?

Tommy never started fights, but was not one to back down either, his protective nature sometimes tipping into recklessness. She wanted to call out, to tell him to just come back inside and call the police, but the set of his shoulders told her he wouldn't listen. Holding her breath, she gripped the curtain, her pulse pounding in her ears as he drove away.

Though she did her best to make herself useful, cleaning the house for the upcoming evening, Rosie couldn't get Tommy out of her mind. Because they were out in the middle of nowhere, she understood why he needed to make sure everything was all right. She knew that Tommy wouldn't be able to relax until he knew she was safe. It was one of the many things she adored about him.

Not being able to really concentrate on her tasks, Rosie

paced back and forth between wiping down the kitchen counters, to peering out the front window. Then back to the kitchen to scour the stove top, and once again to the window. After the third round-trip she felt a bit foolish and decided to stay in the kitchen.

Not ten minutes after he left, she heard the familiar roar of the Jeep engine. Rosie dropped some paper towels onto the counter, which she just realized she had wadded up in a death grip. Shaking the numbness out of her hands as she ran to the front door, she flung it open, just as he reached for the doorknob.

Rosie jumped into Tommy's arms. "Oh my god. I was sure that he had killed you and dumped your body in the woods!" She wrapped her arms around him and squeezed.

"Whoa, whoa, it's okay, I'm fine. You didn't really think I was going to get myself killed, did you? I can handle myself."

Rosie released him and stepped back to get a better look.

His jaw was tight, a faint flicker of tension visible at the hinge. His eyes, steady and unblinking, held a piercing intensity, their depths shadowed with thought. His brows were slightly furrowed, not in anger, but in deep concentration, as if weighing every possibility before speaking. A quiet resolve radiated from him, an unspoken gravity that made it clear— this was not a moment for lightness or hesitation.

She shrugged in response to his question. "I don't know. I was just worried, I guess. Sure, you can handle yourself, but that does you no good when he has a gun, or an axe, or whatever. You didn't have any of that."

Tommy stretched his arms wide, as if embracing the entire world, his smile was warm. "As you can see, I'm perfectly all right. So please just try to relax. Everything is fine."

"So what happened? Did he say why he was lurking out on our road?"

"No, he didn't. In fact, he didn't say anything. He was gone by the time I got there. I looked around, even drove out to the main road, and up a mile or so, but nothing."

Rosie looked down at her feet and frowned.

"What, are you disappointed that I didn't get into a fight, and possibly killed by a hatchet wielding maniac?"

She swatted at his arm. "Stop it. I was really worried about you. And now that whoever that was is gone, we might never know what he wanted."

"Yeah, well, like I told you," Tommy explained, "he was probably just lost and took a wrong turn. The wifi out here is shit, so he probably couldn't get a signal. I bet he's at the gas station in town right now, asking directions."

She shrugged again. "Yeah, maybe."

Late that afternoon, Rosie had relaxed a bit, as there were no more incidences on their road. Tommy was upstairs working and she was getting dinner ready. Sergio and Elena would be arriving shortly.

Rosie moved quickly through the house, lighting candles and fluffing the pillows on the couch, a soft hum escaping her lips as she went. The scent of garlic and rosemary filled the air from the oven, where a tray of roasted vegetables sizzled beside perfectly seared steaks.

She set the table with care—wine glasses polished, cloth napkins folded neatly, the centerpiece a simple vase of fresh flowers she'd sent Tommy out to buy that morning. A playlist of mellow jazz played in the background, filling the space with warmth. Glancing at the clock, she hurried to pour the red wine, just as headlights appeared in the driveway. With a final scan of the cozy scene she had created, she smiled— everything was ready for a perfect evening with their friends.

"Oh my god, what smells so heavenly!" Elena exclaimed as the pair let themselves in.

"Steak and veggies," Rosie told her as the four of them exchanged hugs. "And wine, of course."

"Yes, please." Elena grinned.

Rosie took her hand and led her friend to the dining table. "Here you go. I hope it has had enough time to breathe."

Elena lifted her eyebrows in response, knowing that Rosie was not really a wine connoisseur.

Rosie let out a snicker, as she picked up her own glass. "Oh hell, it's been five minutes. Long enough!" With that, the women clanked glasses and began an evening of laughter and fun.

CHAPTER 7

Laughter bounced off the walls of the cabin.

"Oh my god!" Rosie howled, barely able to contain the laughter inside of her. "Why would you tell them that?!" The wine made her happy and giggly. Wine always made her giggly.

"Because it's true and you know it." Tommy gave her a toothy grin.

"You know what?" she replied. "You are lucky I'm not calling a divorce lawyer after that one."

"Ha ha, very funny. You couldn't do better than me," Tommy retorted.

"Wanna bet?" Rosie's eyes lit up when she smiled.

Rosie Allen was what you would call attractive. Beautiful? Not really. But certainly pleasant to look at. Her slim frame and shoulder length light brown hair paired nicely with her bright blue eyes. At thirty-six years old, she was heading into her forties with not a wrinkle in sight.

Married for fifteen years, she and Tommy had a pretty great marriage. They knew that they could joke around about such things, and the air never got too heavy. The pair had decided early in their relationship that children were not for them. And they thrived because of it. Frequent vacations and lots of travel kept them very entertained.

"Okay okay, you two," Sergio interrupted. "This night is getting out of hand." He looked over at his wife, Elena, who was smiling at all the nonsense.

By any standard Elena Rivera was gorgeous. She had long, jet black hair and deep brown eyes. She was naturally thin and never had to worry about her weight. Though she never got internationally famous, she had graced the pages of quite a few fashion magazines as a teen. Now in her mid-thirties, though still breathtaking, the photographers didn't call so much anymore.

She was okay with it though. Elena loved the simple life. Traveling got old after a while, and she was perfectly happy hanging out in their tiny mountain town. She and Sergio were happily married, and trying for a baby. With any luck, they'd be expecting before the year was out.

The cabin exuded a cozy, rustic charm. The walls were made of rich, textured logs, graced with natural knots and the grain of the wood. A stone fireplace sat prominently against one wall, with a stack of firewood neatly piled nearby, ready to crackle with a warm, inviting fire.

Above the fireplace, there was a wooden mantel holding a photograph of Tommy and Rosie on their wedding day, a few old books, a decorative lantern, and small knick knacks, such as pine cones and forest animal figurines.

The warm, amber-colored shades and a couple of large windows let in natural light during the day. In the evenings, the lamps gave it a nice cozy feeling inside.

Braided rugs and a soft faux bearskin were scattered

about the natural wooden floors. The earthy tones of the furniture gave it just the right cabiny feeling.

The walls were adorned with old photographs, of time gone-by, paintings of forest scenes, and even an old rusty ax. It all added a personal touch that told a story of the cabin's history. The previous owner's family had left most of the decor after his death, as they had no use for rustic mountain odds and ends at their modern big city houses.

One bedroom was down a short hallway, and a staircase led to the second level loft. The simple wooden bed had a thick handmade quilt on it.

An authentic antique stove adorned the kitchen. It did work, but was mostly for show. A standard oven and stove had been installed many years ago, for ease in use.

The open shelves were stocked with dishware featuring moose with red and black checkers around the border. A couple of cast-iron skillets hung on the wall.

The air was filled with the scent of pine, and just a hint of fresh wildflowers, adding to the feeling of being nestled deep in the heart of the woods.

Both couples looked up at the ceiling as the wind scraped a pine tree across the roof.

"What was that?" Rosie asked.

"Probably a squirrel, or maybe even a tree branch. You'll get used to it out here in the boondocks," Sergio explained. "Also, don't be surprised if you hear a pack of coyotes yipping up a storm in the middle of the night. They do that sometimes."

"Yeah, we've heard them. It's kind of unnerving at first," Rosie replied. "But we're getting used to it. Oh, and we saw a bear the other day. It didn't come up to the cabin or anything. It just kind of stayed in the tree line, watching us. After a few minutes, he moved on, I guess. Haven't seen him since."

"I've read that bears can eat up to 90 pounds of food a day when preparing for hibernation, which is probably any time now. So I'm sure he was just looking for food," Sergio told them.

"Well, I don't want to be that food. I'm not leaving this cabin without my bear spray, that's for sure," Rosie told the group.

"We've lived here for years," Sergio told her. "I haven't heard of a single instance where a bear attacked someone. So I wouldn't really worry about it."

Rosie tilted her head as she contemplated what he had just told her. It didn't matter if the bears around Silver Lake were normally aggressive or not, she wasn't taking any chances. Bear spray was always in her pocket.

"Well, I just want to add that I'm glad the two of you moved here. This is fun," Sergio added.

Elena looked at her husband with a smirk, and turned back to their friends. "This guy right here," pointing at Sergio with just her thumb, "I usually have to drag out to do things, especially with other people. You must be working some magic if he is happy that you are here. He told me he was looking forward to tonight."

All three looked over at him, and he he lifted his palms and shoulders, "What? You all are cool with me."

Laughter floated upward.

"More wine please."

Tommy reached over to the wine bottle on the coffee table, lifting it up to eye level. Satisfied that there was just enough left, he took the glass that Rosie was holding out in front of her, and filled it with the last of the bottle.

Rosie took a sip. "This wine is delicious. Where did you get it?" She directed her question to Elena, sitting with Sergio on the couch across from them.

"At the liquor store right in town." Elena tilted her head.

"Well, it's not really just a liquor store. They also sell souvenirs and snacks, and all that type of stuff. More of a general store, I guess." She shrugged. "Anyway, that's where I got it. For a store in a small town like this, they really have a great wine selection. You should check it out sometime."

Rosie nodded. "Yeah, I will. Wine's not usually my go-to drink. I love me a margarita usually. But that may change." She held the glass out in front of her and studied the contents. "We need to stock up on this stuff."

"Whoa, hold your horses there, missy," Tommy smiled and glanced around the room. "This place isn't big enough to be stocking up on anything. But we can go pick up a bottle or two next week, if you like."

His wife laughed. "I like."

CHAPTER 8

"I can't believe you bought this wonderful cabin." Elena's gaze scanned the room. "It's just gorgeous. I'm kind of jealous."

Rosie's cheeks turned just the palest of pink. She shrugged. "Thanks. We got such a great deal, because the family of the previous owner just wanted to unload it after he died."

Elena's breath caught in her throat as the words settled over her like a cold fog. A man may have died here. In *this* house. The walls around her, once warm and inviting, suddenly felt different—heavier. Her pulse quickened, and she swallowed hard, glancing toward the dim hallway, where shadows seemed to stretch a little too far.

Had he died peacefully? Or had something terrible happened? The thought made her skin prickle. She wrapped her arms around herself, trying to shake the uneasy feeling creeping up her spine.

Elena's eyes darted around the room. "He didn't...die in here... did he?"

Rosie waved her hand in the air dismissively. "No, no. He

was some notorious criminal or drug dealer, or something like that. I guess this was his hideout. He got killed somewhere in Sacramento. But really, that's all we know about it."

"In this town, I'm shocked that we hadn't heard about it. I mean, everyone here is kind of all up in everyone's business. It's hard to leave your house without the whole town knowing what you are up to that day," Elena explained. "So how was it even possible that we didn't know about this man?"

"From what we understand, the old man never left this cabin. He holed up here and kept to himself. I guess if he stayed out of sight then no one would really know his business," Tommy told them. "I guess it worked too, because even our real estate agent didn't know anything about him. We had to do our own research."

Sergio jumped in to the conversation. "Yeah, I remember you telling me about that. It's kind of a cool conversation piece."

Elena let out a relaxing breath. "Sorry, I know I'm kind of ridiculous about things sometimes. But just the thought of someone dying in the same place I'm going to sleep in, well… it gives me the heebie-jeebies."

"You know, most places on earth have probably had hundreds, if not thousands, of people die there at some point in the course of history," Tommy told them.

Elena looked at him. "No, that can't be true."

"Yeah, just think about it," he continued. "There have been many billions of people who have died in the last hundred thousand years. So, even though this cabin wasn't always here, obviously, this piece of land was. Indigenous people, visitors, cowboys, hell, maybe even cavemen, I don't really know, but they may have all walked in this forest at one time or another. Chances are pretty good that lots of people have died around here. Maybe right on this very spot."

Everyone in the room looked down at the floor.

"So…I wouldn't worry about it. Tons of people have probably died around your house also. Everywhere really."

Everyone went silent and Tommy looked into each of their faces. "What?"

"Way to make us all freak out," Rosie replied. "Now we have to think about someone dying right here in this spot a thousand years ago."

"It's no big deal. You women can be so jumpy. I mean, people die. It's just the way it is." There was that toothy grin of Tommy's again.

Rosie swatted at him. "Yeah, whatever." Jumping up, she motioned for Elena to follow her. "Come on, let's open another bottle of wine. I'm losing my buzz and I need to forget everything my husband just said to us."

The sound of laughter floated toward the kitchen as they made their way over. Once safely in the kitchen, Elena leaned in, keeping her voice low. "This place really is fantastic, I mean it. And, even though our town is small, you are out here in the middle of nowhere, all secluded. It's cozy and romantic. I wish we had bought something like this." Elena scanned the room, turning in a full circle.

"Yeah," Rosie replied, "since we both can work from home now, there was no reason for us to not move out here permanently, instead of the back and forth to the city. That was killing us. I know we have only been here permanently for a few weeks, but we love it. The area, the forest, the small town, everything is fantastic. I doubt we'll ever leave here."

Rosie grabbed a bottle of red wine from the refrigerator and began the task of opening it.

The two women had met months prior at the Silver Lake gym. Tommy and Rosie hadn't yet purchased their cabin, so they were making frequent trips to Silver Lake, looking for just the right one.

Rosie had asked Elena how much longer she was going to be on the treadmill. They got to talking and became fast friends. After that, they were practically attached at the hip, and spoke on the phone daily. They also synced up their workout routines and saw each other twice a week. That part slowed down after Tommy and Rosie moved out to the cabin, but she managed to still make it to the gym once a week.

Their husbands got to know each other after that, and had also become friends. Though the men rarely saw each other outside of the nights the wives organized for the couples on a fairly regular basis.

"Do you have any more cheese and crackers? Those were really yummy, and if I'm going to have more to drink, I should probably get some more food in my belly," Elena explained. "I get way too out of hand when I'm drunk," she howled.

"Hey, what's so funny in there?" Tommy called from the living room.

"Nothing, don't you worry about it!" Rosie answered back in a lighthearted response.

Rosie turned back to Elena and shook her head. "Men."

Elena smiled at her friend. She just adored the woman. Rosie was outgoing and friendly, someone who people were drawn to. She had never lacked for friends, ever.

Elena, on the other hand, was beautiful, yes, of that there was no doubt. But she was quieter. Kind of shy. People did tend to like her, as she didn't have a mean bone in her body, but they weren't really drawn to her, like they were to Rosie.

"Oh," she pointed. "The crackers are in that cabinet. We have a ton of cheese. Tommy loves his cheese." She laughed at her own words. "I'll get it."

"Naw, I got it." Elena opened the cabinet and pulled out two red and yellow boxes with a picture of the desired snack on the front. "Got 'em," Elena announced. "Here, give me the cheese and I'll make a platter. Where are the knives?"

"In that drawer right in front of you."

Snap!

Elena jumped at the sound and dropped the knife she was holding. It clanked on the floor twice before coming to a stop an inch from her bare feet.

Both women looked at the knife on the floor, then to each other.

"What was that?" Elena asked.

"Something outside," Rosie answered.

They both turned toward the kitchen door.

"An animal?"

"Yeah probably. It has to be. We do get bears out here, but I haven't seen one yet. It was probably just a coyote or raccoon," Rosie told her.

"No way was that a coyote or raccoon," Elena whispered. "It was really loud. Like something heavy. I think it was a bear."

"Why are you whispering?" Rosie asked with a smile. "Whatever it is, it's outside. We're safe in here."

"Are your doors locked?"

CHAPTER 9

"Um no, it's not locked. At least I don't think it is. Bears don't turn doorknobs," Rosie tried to explain to Elena.

"How do you know that? You ever asked one?"

"You know what? The men need to be good for something." Rosie said over her shoulder as she headed for the living room. She found them deep in conversation about some football team. Rosie didn't know one team from another. It was all greek to her.

"Hey you guys," she interrupted. Tommy continued what he was saying and only when done did he stop to look at her. Rosie narrowed her eyes his way. "We heard a noise outside. I think something is stalking around the cabin. It's creeping us out."

"So?" Sergio replied. "It's the forest. There are noises out there. Now that you live here, you can't get freaked out every time you hear something. Otherwise, you'll never leave this cabin. Trust me, it's never anything. Usually just squirrels."

"Serg, it's not squirrels. Trust me. It was something heavy stepping on branches and stuff. Heavy." She made a downward motion with the palms of her hand. "Really heavy. Not some little critters scurrying about," Rosie tried to explain. "It could be a person."

"Rosie, no one is out there. We have no crime around here. I don't know anyone who locks their doors. No one is gonna break in," Tommy told his wife. "That's why we moved here." He turned back to continue the conversation with Sergio, completely disregarding the concern on his wife's face.

"Well, we haven't been here that long," Rosie replied. "I'm from San Francisco, and we keep our doors locked. It's just how it's done. I don't want random strangers just walking into my house. Are you okay with that, cause I don't like it. It freaks me out."

His eyes darted toward her impatiently. His voice was clipped and edged with frustration, as if he were barely holding back a sharp remark. "Then lock the door," Tommy told her.

"Excuse me?" Rosie replied. "Are you serious right now?"

"Come on, honey, we are having a good time here," Tommy told her, not wanting to get up from the couch. The wine had gone to his head and he was unsure how steady he would be on his feet. "Nothing out there is going to knock the door down. Go get Elena and we can all play a game, okay?"

Rosie placed both fists on her hips and raised her eyebrows, without saying a word.

"Aw, come on," Tommy continued. "We are out here in the middle of nowhere. How would someone even find us? No one is gonna go miles out into the forest to find a cabin to break into. Especially one with lights on and obviously has people inside."

"Then it's a bear. I'm telling you, something or someone is out there."

"Okay, maybe it is," he replied. "So if that's the case, I definitely don't want to go out there. You think I want to get ripped to shreds?" He turned to Sergio and smiled.

"Not funny, Tommy. I just want you to go look, that's all. I'm not asking you to fight it."

Her husband took in her stance, and the look on her face. Resigned, he set his glass down in front of him and climbed up off the couch, hanging onto the arm to steady himself. "Yeah, yeah, okay. I'm going." He looked over at Sergio. "You coming? Don't make me face the big bad raccoon all by myself."

Sergio grinned, following Tommy. He grabbed the baseball bat that Tommy kept by the front door, slinging it over his shoulder. "Let's do this."

"It isn't a raccoon!" Rosie called after them. "It sounded huge, like a grizzly bear. Or maybe even Bigfoot. I don't know what it is."

"Come on, woman, you know there are no grizzlies, or Bigfoots...Bigfeet?" he laughed, "around here." Tommy slammed the door behind them.

Tommy left a hesitant Sergio standing on the wooden deck, looking out into the pitch black night. "Hurry up," Tommy told Sergio, who finally decided to jog over and walk next to him.

"I know we've lived in the mountains for a while now," Sergio told him, "but I've never liked how freaking dark it gets around here at night. You can't see three feet in front of..."

Tommy held up his hand, in a stopping motion. "Wait, did you hear that?" he whispered.

A soft rustling in the leaves was the only sound as they moved cautiously along the tree line. The air was crisp, with a slight breeze stirring the high branches. Suddenly, the quiet was broken by an unmistakable *crunch*—the sound of something heavy stepping on brittle twigs and dried leaves nearby.

They froze, heart pounding, ears straining to catch more. Another crunch, closer this time, as if something was moving just out of sight in the shadows. The sound was slow and deliberate, like something big shifting its weight. Each step echoed through the dense woods, amplifying the mystery and hinting at the unknown presence lurking just beyond the tree line.

"What the hell is that?!" Tommy yelled out.

"Shhh," Sergio whispered. "We don't want to alert it to our position."

Tommy's eyes grew wide. "*It*? What is out here, Serg?"

Returning to the kitchen, Rosie grumbled about the men. "Did you hear them laughing at me? I should…"

"Shhh, I heard that sound again," Elena told her. "There is definitely something out there. I'm locking the door. I'm sure there are some animals that can open it."

"It's probably just the guys out there walking around that you heard. At least I hope so," Rosie told her.

"Well, I'm not taking any chances. When they come back and knock, I'll let them in. In the meantime, I don't know what the hell is out there."

Elena walked to the exterior kitchen door and reached to lock the deadbolt. Just as she did, the doorknob turned. Her hand bolted from the handle and both women screamed.

CHAPTER 10

The two strangers pushed in, their heavy boots thudding against the tiled floor. Dressed head to toe in black, with ski masks obscuring their faces, only their eyes—cold and unreadable—were visible. The dim light caught the gleam of the handguns they brandished, their grips firm and unwavering.

A tense silence gripped the room, the air thick with fear as the intruders scanned their surroundings, their intent clear yet unspoken. Every movement was calculated, every second stretched, as those caught in their path held their breath, waiting for what would come next.

Terrified of making a sound, the women backed up. "What the..."

The shorter man spoke first, interrupting Rosie's words, his voice low. "Don't make a sound or we will kill you. Got it?" His eyes darted between the women.

Both Rosie and Elena nodded as they backed into the kitchen counter, stopping their progress.

"You." The shorter man pointed at Rosie as he pulled a zip

tie from his pants pocket. "Turn around and put your hands behind your back."

"Please don't hurt us," Rosie pleaded.

The man backhanded her across the face. "Didn't I tell you not to make a sound?"

Rosie nodded her head quickly, a single tear slid down her cheek.

"Now turn around."

She did as she was told. The taller man hadn't said a word. He just stood behind the shorter man with his gun pointed at the women. Elena noticed that he kept glancing over at the door to the living room.

"Where are your husbands? Are they in there?" the taller man finally asked, tilting his head toward the door.

"We heard a noise outside," Rosie replied. "I guess that was you."

"Yeah, you think?" the shorter man replied, disdain dripping from his voice.

He connected the ends and pulled the zip tie tightly around Rosie's wrists. She winced.

"It's too tight."

"Shut up. You'll live," the man told her, turning his attention toward Elena, "Now you, sweet thing. Turn around and put your hands behind your back."

Elena complied without complaint. Once done, he turned them both around, facing the men.

"So are your husbands outside right now?" he asked them.

"Yes," Rosie replied.

The shorter man looked over at Elena. His eyes scraped over her body from the top of her head to her bare feet, pausing at her breasts momentarily, as he checked out every inch of her.

Elena could physically feel his eyes on her. Her heart began pounding in her throat.

"You haven't said a word. Anything to add?" he asked her.

"I'm just being quiet, like you told us to," she replied.

"Good girl."

He reached over and caressed her neck. She stiffened at his touch and turned her head away from him.

"Don't you touch her," Rosie told him.

Dante pulled his hand from Elena's neck and got within three inches of Rosie's face. They were the same height and she could see his dull brown eyes piercing into her from behind the ski mask.

"Shut up or I'll gut her right here and now, while you watch." It was said through clenched teeth, and he seemed to hiss the words out. "Then, when I'm done with her, I'm going to take out my frustrations on your husband. It has been a while since I've shot anyone between the eyes. It might be fun target practice."

He smiled and Rosie held in a shuddering breath. "Understood?"

Rosie quickly nodded her head.

"Yeah, that's what I thought." He turned to Angelo. "Keep an eye on this one, will ya?"

"I don't work for you, remember?" Angelo replied.

Dante ignored his partner's words and turned his attentions back to the beautiful brunette standing next to the mouthy one.

"What is your name, sweet thing?"

Elena bit her top lip, not wanting to give him any information about herself.

Her eyes widened as he stepped closer, his voice low and insistent. "I asked you a question."

She could feel her pulse hammering in her throat, her breath shallow and uneven, as her head swam with the effects of the wine.

He asked again, his tone growing sharper, but she

couldn't make herself speak. Instead, she shook her head, small and hesitant at first, then more firmly as she tried to take a shaky step back, pressing into the cabinet with every bit of herself that she could. Her hands trembled, still in the zip ties, fingers curling into fists, but she didn't dare look away. She just kept shaking her head, silently pleading, hoping he would understand—hoping he would stop.

Before anyone realized what was happening, in one swift move, Dante pulled a knife out of a sheath attached to his belt and slid the pointy end lightly across Rosie's cheek. A red streak formed and a single droplet of blood dribbled down her face.

Elena gasped. Rosie never said a word.

He turned back to Elena. "Now, are you going to answer my question or not?"

Elena looked over at her friend, and whispered, "I'm sorry."

"I'm fine, honey. It's nothing."

She looked at the short man in front of her and narrowed her eyes. "It's...Elena." Her words were shaky.

"See, now was that so hard, Elena?" Dante slowly replied. "That's a beautiful name, by the way. It sounds exotic." His eyes travelled down her body once more. "Like you."

She didn't dare respond.

Elena tensed as his fingers brushed the side of her neck once again, a shiver running through her that had nothing to do with warmth. His touch was slow, deliberate, trailing down the curve of her throat to her collarbone, then lower, pausing between her breasts for just a bit too long.

Elena flinched. She wanted to recoil, to shrink away, but her body felt frozen, locked in place by fear. She had nowhere to go. Her breath hitched as his hand lingered, his fingertips barely pressing into her skin, a silent reminder of his control. She swallowed hard, her pulse pounding in her ears, every instinct screaming for her to run—but she couldn't.

His hand began gliding over her chest and toward her stomach.

"Hey man," the taller of the two said, "that's enough. Leave her alone. We have more important things to worry about right now." His eyes kept watch on the door leading to the living room, even as he watched what Dante was doing.

"Shut up, Angelo, and mind your own business." The shorter man never took his eyes off of Elena. "Just watch the door."

"Dante, what the fuck? You just said my name."

"And you just said mine, dumbass. I guess we are out in the open now," Dante, the shorter of the two, laughed. "It doesn't matter anyway. They aren't going to tell anyone. Now are you, honey?" He caressed her cheek and slender neck as he spoke.

Elena turned her head away once more and kept her mouth shut. She was in no position to complain. She only prayed that their husbands would return soon, so this nightmare would end. Her head was still swimming from a bit too much wine. She cursed that fact, wishing that she had remained sober that evening.

The front door of the cabin opened, bringing in with it the laughter of two intoxicated men. One had just told a joke and apparently it was the funniest thing either of them had ever heard.

"Hey Rosie! Where are you? We took care of the big bad wolf," Tommy called toward the kitchen.

Dante looked toward the living room door, and back to the women. He placed his index finger over his lips and leaned in. "Not a word."

The look on his face told the women he meant business.

Both were terrified that he would kill their husbands. Neither one made a sound.

"Hey, where are you guys?" Tommy headed toward the kitchen, with Sergio in tow.

Pushing open the swinging door, the men came face to face with the two ski masks.

"What the..."

CHAPTER 11

Elena witnessed the tall man slam his gun into her husband's head. A dull, heavy thunk seemed to reverberate around the room, and Elena could have sworn that she heard a crack when the gun made contact. Sergio landed on the kitchen floor, and unconsciousness overcame him before anyone comprehended what had just happened.

Before anyone had the chance to react, Angelo and Dante pointed their guns at the heads of the husbands.

"Sergio!" Elena screamed. Her fear was palpable.

"Don't move." Angelo said it with such authority that Tommy's hands shot up in the air in front of him.

Tommy glanced over at his wife. His gaze was fixed and wide, almost frozen. Her eyes looked as if she were pleading for a way out, silently shouting what her voice could not express. It broke his heart. He noticed what looked like a knife cut across her cheek, still bleeding lightly. It hurt him that someone hurt her.

A groan from the floor turned all eyes his way. Sergio was regaining consciousness. His hand went immediately to the side of his head with the wound on it. He felt the warm liquid slowly oozing from his head. He looked up to find everyone watching him intently, his eyes darting from person to person.

"Are you okay, baby?" Sergio asked his wife, while still lying on the floor.

Dante turned and narrowed his eyes at her. She only nodded in response to her husband.

"This is your wife?" Dante asked Sergio. "Man oh man, who knew you could land a looker like this? She's way out of your league." He looked her up and down once more. "I bet she's a wildcat between the sheets."

"Shut up about my wife!" It took everything he had for Sergio to struggle to his feet. "Don't talk about her like that." His eyes were narrowed and he spoke through gritted teeth. "I'll kill…"

"Okay enough. Back up," Angelo told the husbands. "Into the living room." He turned to his partner. "You keep an eye on the women in here. And keep your hands to yourself."

Tommy and Sergio backed through the door the way they had come. Angelo following them closely, his gun held steady. He pulled a couple of zip ties from his pocket that Dante had given him before they entered the house.

"Here." He threw them at Sergio. "You tie up your friend here and then I'll tie you up."

Tommy began to lower his hands. "Now wait a minute. What is this all about? We don't have anything of value here. We just moved in…"

"Shut up!" Angelo told him. "Turn around and put your hands behind your back so he can tie you up. And if you keep running your mouth, I have duct tape with me."

"Okay, okay," Tommy replied.

Sergio kept quiet as he reached for the zip ties. His head was pounding. It felt as if the butt of that gun had split his head wide open.

Tommy turned around and let Sergio tie up his hands. He made them tighter than they needed to be. But Tommy didn't say a word. His priority at the moment was to make sure that Rosie and Elena were okay. He was terrified of what the other man was doing in the kitchen only a few feet away.

"Okay, you turn around now, and put your hands behind your back," Angelo ordered Sergio.

Once Tommy and Sergio were both tied up, Angelo directed them to sit on the couch. The men did as they were told.

"Hey Dante, bring the chicks in!" he called to the kitchen.

No response.

"Dante! Did you hear me? Get in here!"

It took two full minutes before the trio emerged from the kitchen, with Rosie leading the way. She was followed by Elena, then Dante.

"What the hell took you so long?" Angelo asked his partner.

The only response Dante gave him was an almost imperceptible smile.

Angelo directed the women to sit on the couch with the men.

"Are you okay?" Tommy asked Rosie, and she nodded.

"Did I tell you that you could talk?" Dante asked him.

"I'm just making sure my wife is okay." Tommy's reply was defiant.

"Don't speak to each other. From now on, you only speak to us. Got it?"

"What is going on here?" Tommy asked. "Why are you doing this?"

"Because you have something we need," Dante sneered.

Tommy's eyes darted around the room. "What are you talking about? What could we possibly have that you want? We don't really have anything of value here."

"Never you mind." He turned to his partner. "Hey, why don't you go get the tools from out back?"

Angelo left the room without a word.

"What do you need tools for?" Tommy asked, his voice shaky.

Dante only stared back at him, ignoring the question.

Dante addressed the four people on the couch in front of him. "Don't any of you move, because I don't have a problem shooting any of you. I just got this gun and have been dying to try it out." He used his left hand to caress the top of the gun. "Isn't it beautiful?"

No one responded.

It took a good five minutes before Angelo returned.

"What the hell took you so long?" Dante asked as Angelo lugged in two sledgehammers and two large duffle bags.

The group on the couch all looked at each other. "What are you going to do with…those things?" Tommy choked out, fearing that the sledgehammers and duffle bags were meant for them.

Dante laughed. He knew what Tommy was getting at. "Don't you worry, sport. We have more important things going on here. You just stay right there and keep your mouth shut." He turned to Angelo. "Keep your gun on them. If anyone moves, shoot 'em."

CHAPTER 12

Dante placed his gun on the fireplace mantel and looked over at the couch. "Don't get any bright ideas. My friend here isn't afraid to kill you."

Angelo looked over and smiled. It was true. Killing didn't bother him. Most of the time anyway. He had killed many people for the boss, over the past few years. The job paid well, and he appreciated that. This job alone was worth about a hundred grand to each of them. That would set him up for a good while.

Dante picked up one of the sledgehammers. "Damn, this thing is heavy. It could bash a head into smithereens with one blow." He glanced over at the couch.

Elena cried out.

"Oh don't you worry your pretty little head, sweet cheeks," Dante told her. "I have other plans for you."

Elena's wide eyes were pleading with her husband.

"Watch your mouth!" Sergio yelled. "If you touch my wife, I will kill you."

"Who has the guns and sledgehammers here? Me or you? You are not in charge. I am. Keep that in mind."

"I will kill you with my bare hands," Sergio responded, his jaw tensed.

Dante laughed at the threat from the man tied up. He walked over, still holding the sledgehammer and used the business end of it to point right at Sergio's head. Sergio took in a deep breath and held it, expecting the worst.

"You got anything else to say, sport? Anything at all?"

Sergio shook his head, without uttering a word. He knew that the men had the upper hand. His threats would get him nowhere.

"Man, what are you doing? Have you lost your mind?" Angelo asked his partner. "Don't mess with him, otherwise the Boss will take it out on us later."

Dante looked over at Angelo and turned back to Sergio, smiling. "Just fooling around."

He dropped the sledgehammer to his side and turned toward the wall next to the fireplace. Inspecting it, he ran his hand as far up as he could, stopping when he noticed two picture frames with magazine covers in them. The model was beautiful and young. Looked to be a teenager to him. "Who is...oh."

He turned and looked at Elena Rivera. His face stuck in a smile. "Is this you?"

She nodded, ever so slightly.

Rosie immediately regretted hanging the magazine covers of Elena on their wall. She was proud of her friend, and loved that she used to be famous. In her wildest dreams she could never have imagined this scenario playing out.

"Well well, ladies and gentlemen, we have a celebrity amongst us." Dante caressed the photos on the wall. "Damn girl, you were hot." He looked over at her. "You still are."

"Leave her alone!" Sergio yelled.

"You know what, sport? You don't get to tell me what to do." He lifted the sledgehammer. "Just test me."

Sergio averted his eyes.

"Yeah, that's what I thought."

Dante turned back to the wall to continue what he had been doing. He rubbed his hand from the photos all the way to where the wall and floor met, knocking on it a couple of times.

"If I'm not mistaken, I do believe this is what we're looking for. Only one way to find out for sure."

He lugged the sledgehammer over his right shoulder and swung with everything he had, hitting the wall with a thunderous bang. The family photos on the fireplace mantel tumbled down into a heap on the floor, shattering the glass in the process. A large chunk of drywall crumbled, leaving behind a gaping hole the size of a basketball.

"What the hell are you doing?" Tommy yelled. "That's my wall!"

"Well, you are about to find out," Dante replied, taking another swing with the sledgehammer. Another large chunk of the wall caved in.

"Stop!" Tommy yelled again, temporarily forgetting their predicament and thinking of nothing more than the fact that he and Rosie were going to have to pay to get the wall fixed.

Dante ignored the outburst, set the sledgehammer on the floor next to him, and bent over to peer into the hole that was now about two feet in diameter. He howled with satisfaction.

Reaching in, Dante pulled out a fistful of hundred dollar bills. "Now that's what I'm talking about!"

"What the hell?" Tommy exclaimed. "How did that get in there?"

"How do you think it got in there?" Angelo responded. "The old man who used to own this place needed somewhere to hide it from the feds, so he put it there. It worked too, cause no one knew where to find it." He smiled. "Except us.

We are the only ones with the balls to actually come here and find it for ourselves."

Dante swung the sledgehammer a few more times, revealing what looked like millions of dollars hidden inside the wall. It was stacked neatly between the framing boards.

Tommy and Rosie wondered how in the world someone could put all that money into the wall, re-drywall it, paint it, and no one knew about it. Clearly their realtor, and the family they bought it from didn't know. Otherwise they would have taken it. There was way more money in that wall than the house was worth.

"My shoulders are starting to ache. Your turn." Dante dropped the sledgehammer to the floor with a thud.

He picked up his gun from the fireplace mantel, brushing off the drywall chunks and dust that had landed on it.

Angelo wasted no time getting to work. Being a big guy, Angelo made short work of the remaining drywall. The scene in front of them was nothing short of magnificent.

The two men cheered, while the four hostages sat stone faced on the couch.

"You two." Dante pointed at Tommy and Rosie with his gun. "Get up."

"Why?" Rosie asked in just the softest of voices.

She was terrified, they all were. Now that the men had their money, there was no reason for them to keep the four of them alive. In fact, she knew that it would be in their best interest to get rid of the witnesses.

"Because I said so. Now get the fuck up!"

They both squirmed their way off the couch, which was not an easy task while their hands were tied behind their backs.

"Turn around," Angelo told them. He cut off the zip ties. "Don't try anything funny."

Rosie rubbed each of her wrists. "We won't. We just want

you to take the money and go. We don't want to be involved in whatever this is. At all."

"That's the plan. Now that we are done with the fun part, grab those duffle bags and fill them with the money," Dante ordered.

Tommy and Rosie did as they were told, while Sergio and Elena looked on. When all was said and done, the two large duffle bags were full to the brim with the cash. There was easily a couple million dollars in them.

"Grab them and let's go," Angelo told them. "Our car is parked out back, just past the group of trees. We need to get out of here."

"Wait," Dante responded. "I have a better idea."

CHAPTER 13

Dante's eyes traveled over to the couch and landed squarely on Elena Rivera. After seeing the look in his face, she slumped further into the soft cushions.

He spoke directly to Angelo, without taking his eyes off of Elena. "Ang, tie these two back up." He pointed at Tommy and Rosie. "I have something I need to do first."

"What do you need to do?" Angelo asked. "We got the money. That's what we came for." He looked around, not understanding what was going on.

"Don't worry about it. Just do as I say."

"Get in, get out, don't muck around. That's what we are here for. And only that," Angelo reminded him.

The look on Dante's face caused Angelo to go silent. Yes, Dante was almost a foot shorter than him, but the man could be intimidating. Especially when he was focused on something. Angelo knew this all too well. And he saw Dante's interest in the pretty one. That terrified him.

Angelo was conflicted. On the one hand, he could just leave Dante there, and let the man face having to deal with four people on his own. On the other hand, if he did that,

Dante would probably come after him. And when the man was pissed as you, you better be hiding. He had no qualms about killing anyone who got in his way.

Then there was the third hand. Elena Rivera was someone they should not be messing with. The Boss wouldn't like it. In fact, he might kill Dante himself once he finds out. That put Angelo in the line of fire...a place he didn't want to be.

Dante waved his gun in Angelo's direction. "Just do it."

Angelo did as he was told. But this was the last time. He was done working with Dante. The Boss was just going to have to figure out how to make it work. But, after Dante's behavior tonight, Angelo wasn't so sure that Dante would be around long to worry about. It was just a gut feeling he had.

Once all four people were securely back on the couch, Dante continued.

"You, Miss Fashion Magazine, get up," he ordered.

"What? Me? Why?" The words were meek.

"Uh, hey man, what are you doing?" Angelo asked, knowing full well what the answer was. Dante didn't have a great track record when it came to women.

"I'm doing what I want. You got a problem with that?" His eyes bore into Angelo, who slid his eyes toward Elena and Sergio.

"Um, the boss is going to have a big problem with that," Angelo told him.

"Well, the boss will just have to get over it. I'm tired of his b.s. anyway."

"You stay away from my wife, or I'll kill you!" Sergio yelled.

"Yeah, I don't think you will. You are tied up and can't do anything about it. Now Missy, I'm not going to tell you again to get up." His teeth were clenched as he spoke.

"I don't want to," Elena told him, leaning toward her

husband. She needed Sergio's reassurance that he wouldn't let anything happen to her.

The look on his face told her what she already knew, that he he couldn't do anything about what was next.

In about half a second, Dante crossed the room and grabbed Elena by her arm, yanking her to her feet.

"Do what I say and this will go a lot easier for you. Got it?"

Elena nodded, a single tear dribbled down her cheek.

"I told you to stay away from my wife!" Sergio's face was beet red and spittle flew from his lips.

Dante lazily looked over at Sergio. "Man, you are tied up. What are you going to do about it?"

Sergio began to struggle his way off of the couch. Dante walked over and slammed his gun into the side of the man's head. Blood gushed from the open wound. Both women cried out.

"Leave him alone! I'll do whatever you want," Elena told him. "Just don't hurt him, please."

"Elena, no." Sergio's words were pleading and not as strong as they were just moments prior. His head throbbed and the blood flowed down the side of his face.

Dark red drops of blood splattered onto Sergio's shirt, staining the pale fabric in uneven, jagged patterns. The fresh blood glistened briefly before soaking into the material, spreading slightly and leaving irregular, feathery edges around each mark.

The vivid crimson against the shirt told a silent story of pain, raw and immediate, the marks an undeniable reminder of the violence or injury he had just endured. Another blow to the head might just be the undoing of Sergio Rivera.

Sergio ignored the dripping blood. "You can't keep me tied up forever. When this is all done, I'm going to kill you." His words were slow and deliberate.

Dante had no doubt that Sergio meant what he said.

He didn't care.

Sergio's wife had to be the most beautiful woman Dante had ever met. With that beautifully tanned skin, long shapely legs, perfectly shaped lips, and cascading black hair, he couldn't take his eyes off of her. She exuded sexuality, and when she looked at him with those deep brown eyes of hers, well...he was just putty.

He grinned at her husband through his ski mask. "Your wife and I are gonna have some fun tonight." Dante was poking the bear, and he knew it. It didn't matter at this point. The damage had already started. He figured 'what the hell,' he might as well have a good time.

Sergio didn't respond. He knew there was absolutely nothing he could do about it. One man had his wife, the other had a gun pointed directly at him.

"Dante, don't do this," Angelo said. "This isn't going to end well. You know that. She's not worth it."

"She is to me," he replied. Dante nudged Elena in the back with his gun. "Come on, let's go. Down the hall."

"Elena!" Sergio yelled, as he watched the man follow his wife toward the bedroom at the end of the hallway. His voice was choked with emotion. He turned and buried his face into the couch cushion behind him.

CHAPTER 14

"How can you let that happen? Are you that much of a monster?" Rosie asked Angelo directly.

He averted his eyes.

"Hey! I'm talking to you," she continued. "I thought you two were just here to get the money. But that's not really it, is it?" she goaded. "Is this what you two are all about? Assaulting women while they are tied up and can't defend themselves? Making their husbands go through the emotional torture of knowing what is happening, without being able to do anything about it?" She waited for an answer. None came.

"What kind of a disgusting human being are you? Was this your plan all along? You planned to come in here, tie us up, get the money, and then assault us? Do you have a girlfriend, or even a mother or a sister? How would you feel if someone did that to one of them?"

Angelo met her eyes. "Stop with the questions! No, that was not the plan." He glanced over at Elena's husband, who still had his face buried, doing his best to block out what was happening down the hall. "This is all his doing. I have nothing to do with it."

"Well I think you do," Rosie told him. "You are standing here, aiming a loaded gun at all of us, while god only knows what your partner is doing in the other room." She wasn't backing down. "No, I take that back. We all know exactly what he is doing in the other room. Don't we?"

Angelo's eyes darted to the entrance of the hallway. There was only silence from the other end of the cabin.

"It's not me." Angelo wasn't entirely sure why he felt the need to defend himself to these people. He did not know them, but he did feel like he needed them to know he was not involved in the types of things Dante did.

He was only there for the money, and that was it. He didn't condone any part of what Dante was doing with that woman.

"Then why don't you go down there and do something? Stop him before he goes too far," Rosie suggested. "At this point, all you have done is tie us up and taken some money. We don't care about the money. You can have it, and we'll never bring it up again. But if that man," she tilted her head toward the back bedroom, "if he does what I think he is about to do, then it's going to be too late. And you'll be just as much to blame. Can you live with yourself if that happens? You can go to prison for many years if you let that happen." The woman was not mincing words.

"What he does is his own business. I'm staying out of it," Angelo told her.

"What a piece of shit you are." Tommy finally chimed in. "Both of you."

"Hey, if you don't want to do anything about it, then let me," Rosie told him.

Angelo looked over at her. "You? What do you think you are going to do about it? You think you are just going to walk in there and have a calm conversation with him and he'll just go, 'Oh, okay, you make a lot of sense. I won't rape her now.' Is that what you think is going to happen?"

"I don't know what's going to happen," Rosie responded. "I just know that us all sitting here waiting isn't going to do anything. So if you won't go, then let me. I need to try. Please."

"He'll kill you."

"Yeah, maybe he will. And maybe he won't," she told him. "But if I just sit here and do nothing, and don't even try, then none of it matters. She's my friend, and she's Sergio's wife. Come on, you didn't come here to be involved in this, did you? Tell me the truth, you just want the money and want to go home, right?"

Angelo nodded.

"That's what I thought. So let me try to do something," Rosie asked again.

"I can't do that."

Rosie stared straight into his eyes. "Yes you can."

Angelo didn't respond.

"Are you afraid of him?"

"I'm not afraid of him, and if you don't shut up right now, I'm going to shoot you myself. Dante won't need to."

"Rosie, stop," Tommy told her in a whisper. "You are making things worse."

"How can I make things worse? You do understand what is happening in the other room to our friend right now, don't you?" she asked her husband.

"Yes, of course. But if you don't stop, he's going to kill you. And us. All of us. So just let it go," he told her.

"Tommy, you can't be serious. I need to do what I can to help her."

"That's enough!" Angelo shouted. "Shut the hell up or I'm going to put a bullet through your forehead. Any questions?"

Rosie's lips tightened into a straight line and she buried her face into Tommy's shoulder. The fact that she could do absolutely nothing to help her friend would haunt her until her dying day.

If they survived this ordeal, Rosie knew things would never be the same. Elena and Sergio would not ever come to their house again, and who could blame them? She knew that their friendship was probably over, as it would never leave their minds and they would be reminded every single time they saw each other. Of that, there was no doubt.

The four people in the living room sat silently, expecting to hear a scuffle from down the hall. But they were met with only silence.

"Why is it so quiet? That worries me even more," Rosie asked.

Angelo glared at her.

CHAPTER 15

The first thing Dante noticed as they entered the bedroom was the scent. It consisted of pine trees and cinnamon. The red candle he spotted on the nightstand was the cinnamon culprit. He was unsure where the pine scent came from, but probably just from being in the forest. They may not have added anything to make it smell pine-like.

Ugh, he couldn't wait to get out of the damn mountains, and back to the normal city smells.

Elena's tears spilled down her face. Dante was used to it. Women were so emotional. He gave them a good time, he knew he did. But they never seemed to appreciate him. Even his girlfriend wasn't always up for fun. She wasn't going to be around much longer anyway. He was ready to move on.

Transferring the gun from his right hand to his left, he pulled out the knife on his hip and told her to turn around. "I need to get these ties off of you so we can both enjoy ourselves."

Happy to get the zip ties off, she turned and he sliced through them in one quick flash. Replacing the knife in the sheath, he transferred the gun back to his right hand and used his free hand to turn her back around to face him.

"Take off your clothes," Dante ordered as he closed the bedroom door behind him with a swipe of his foot.

"Please don't do this." Elena's voice quivered, as did her whole body.

He waved the gun back-and-forth in the air in front of him. "Do it. Now." Dante kept his voice steady. "I haven't got all night."

"No."

Dante tilted his head and let out a little chuckle.

He took a step closer to her. "What did you just say?"

Elena stepped back, bumping into the footboard of the pine bed. She looked down to see what she had hit. When she looked back up, he was a foot closer to her.

"Please don't hurt me."

"I don't plan to hurt you, baby. We are going to have fun. I promise that you'll enjoy it."

Elena felt the wine come back up and land in the back of her throat. It was all she could do to keep it down. "I would like you to leave now. I swear that if you just go, I'll never say a word about this night. Just take the money and go." She added "please" for good measure.

Another chuckle escaped Dante's lips. "That's not going to happen. While my friend out there keeps an eye on your husband and buddies, you and I are going to have some fun of our own. Then, when that's over, and only when over, will we take the money and go. So see, sweetheart, I can have both, and there's not a damn thing you can do about it."

Elena scooted along the footboard of the bed, rounding it and ending up between the wall and the far side of the bed. The night stand was up against the bed on one side, and the wall on the other. She was boxed in.

There was a window next to her, and for a moment she

contemplated crashing right through it to escape. But she knew that wouldn't work. How was she even going to get enough leverage to get through the window in the first place from where she stood? Even then, she would probably need to stand on the bed and leap through it.

Visions of her crashing through the window and having every inch of her sliced up from shards of glass danced through her head. No, that wasn't going to work. She needed to figure out a better plan.

"You know, there's only so far you can go. You can't get away," he taunted.

Dante followed her. "If you aren't going to undress yourself, I guess I'll have to do it for you."

"Please don't do this." Her words were unsteady.

Ignoring her desperate pleas, Dante reached up to unbutton her blouse with his left hand. Elena knew that it was now or never. If she waited, she might never again be in a position to defend herself. She was a good seventy-five pounds or so lighter than Dante was. Her only chance was the element of surprise.

He got two buttons undone before she reached for the gun.

"What the…"

Elena slammed his hand up in the air, and grabbed onto the gun before he could pull the trigger.

The fight was on.

The living room filled with palpable tension, as Angelo continued to stand with his gun pointed at the three terrified individuals, their faces etched with fear. The faint sound of muffled cries and scuffling from the bedroom added a chilling layer to the oppressive silence. Elena's desperate pleas piercing the air. The stark contrast between the eerie stillness in one room and the horrific chaos in the other painted a harrowing picture of control and brutality, as the captives could do nothing but bear witness to the unfolding nightmare.

Each of them grabbed onto the gun with both hands and struggled. When Dante yanked it, in an attempt to jar it from her hands, she had the gun in a death grip and they both fell sideways onto the bed. There was no way that she was going to let it go. If she did, the results could prove to be disastrous. He would kill her, and she had no doubt about that.

"Bitch, let it go!"

"You're gonna have to kill me before that happens!" she yelled back, a slight quiver in her voice.

Elena lifted her legs and pressed her feet against the wall for leverage. It was working. He didn't seem to have as good a grip on the weapon as she did. His hands were sweaty and slipping. Perhaps it was her determination, but there was nothing that would get her to let go. It was that or die.

During the struggle, Elena spotted an iron bear statue on the nightstand. It took some doing, but she managed to maneuver just enough, a couple inches at a time, to be able to reach it. Releasing the gun with her right hand, she reached over, stretched to her maximum limit, grabbed a hold of the statue, and with everything she had slammed him in the head with it.

She had been unable to hit him directly. It ended up being more of a glancing blow. Either way, it put a gash in his head. She lost her grip on the iron bear and the gun. The bear hit the wall and clanked on the wooden floor, before coming to a complete stop.

"Son of a bitch!" Dante yelled, dropping the gun, and reaching for his head. The gun landed on the bed.

Before he realized what was going on, Elena lunged for the gun. She was quicker than he was. Standing up, she pointed it at his chest.

While holding the side of his head, as blood oozed

between his fingers, Dante held up his other hand, palm facing the woman. "I'm sorry. I didn't mean it. I swear that I would never have hurt you."

"You're a liar. You were going to rape me."

"No, no, I would've never actually done it. I just wanted to scare you and your friends a bit. That's not me. Ask Angelo out there. He knows I would never hurt a woman."

"I don't believe you. Now back up." She used the gun to motion him to move.

He took two steps back. "What are you going to do?"

"I'm going to take you into the living room and tie you and him up. Then I'm going to call the police. You and your friend out there are going to spend the next several years in prison."

"For what? I didn't actually do anything to you?"

"Are you kidding me? You came here, tied us up, molested me, then bashed in the walls of this cabin? Then, the worst part is that you attacked me. The only reason I'm not lying there," she indicated the bed with a tilt of her head, "broken and bleeding, is that I got the best of you."

"Bitch, you will never get the best of me. And I will never go back to prison."

"It's prison...or you die right here. I'll even let you choose. So, which one is it?"

"I'm gonna kill you." He lunged for Elena.

Those were the last words Dante ever said.

CHAPTER 16

The four people in the living room all jumped at the sound of the gunshot. Sergio whipped his head around and faced the direction of the sound.

Angelo was the first to speak. "What the hell?"

Sergio squirmed to get himself off the couch, while still being bound with zip ties behind his back.

"Hey partner, where do you think you're going?" Angelo asked him.

"I need to go see if my wife is all right!" Sergio yelled.

"You stay here, okay? I'll go check." Angelo made sure that Sergio settled back into the couch before he headed for the back bedroom. He turned back twice to make sure everyone was staying put on the couch.

Turning the corner in the hall, toward the bedroom, Angelo came face to face with Elena Rivera.

Her hair was no longer sleek and shiny down her back. Now it was disheveled and matted, sticking out in all directions. Her face had a spattering of blood droplets, as well as a couple of scratches. Her clothing was askew, and had even more blood on it.

But those things were not what he noticed first. It was the gun pointing directly at his chest. And two shaky hands holding it. Her piercing eyes told him the story of what had probably happened in the bedroom behind her.

"Whe…where's Dante?" he sputtered out.

"You know where he…is." Her voice was just as shaky. "He's dead."

Angelo was still holding his gun, but it was at his side. Nerves rattled throughout his body. With the wild look in Elena's eyes, he didn't dare lift the gun. She looked like she would have no qualms about pulling the trigger if she felt threatened. Instead, he lifted his left hand and faced his palm toward her. It was intended to be a calming gesture.

"Okay, okay. I'm sure he deserved that." Angelo would have said anything right then to get the woman to lower her gun. He never liked Dante, but was conflicted on whether his death was warranted or not. Then again, he doubted Dante was redeemable.

"Now, everything's okay. I'm not here to hurt you. Can you please put your gun down? We can talk, okay?"

His words were soft and soothing. Anything to diffuse the situation. The woman looked a bit crazed and he suddenly feared for his life.

"He…he…that man…" Elena couldn't get the words out.

"I know," he continued with his voice low. "Whatever happened in there is over. You killed him?" His eyebrows lifted automatically while waiting for her response. He knew what her answer would be. Angelo just needed to keep her talking and calm her down.

Elena's head nodded quickly. "You came here with him."

"Yeah, yeah, I know. But I'm not him," Angelo tried to explain.

"You are the same."

"No, I'm not. I only here came for the money. I would never hurt you. I haven't touched you, have I?"

His eyes were filled with raw emotion, mixed with desperation. He felt vulnerable to the traumatized woman holding the gun on him.

"Please don't shoot me. I have a family. A wife and kids."

The gun shook in her hand. "I don't believe you." Elena took a step closer to him.

Angelo held his breath and closed his eyes. He knew what was coming. But after several seconds, nothing happened. He slowly opened his eyes.

He bent down toward the floor. "Look, I'm putting the gun down, slowly. I'm not a killer. I don't assault women. I'm sorry for what he put you through." He softly laid the gun on the floor at his feet, not wanting to startle her. Standing up, he took a step back.

Elena matched his step, closing the distance he had just made between them. She stood silently, the gun still pointing at his chest.

"Please lower the gun. I will leave and never bother you again. I will leave the money, and I can even take Dante with me, if you like. No one will ever know we were here," he pleaded.

"You have to pay for what you've done to me."

Angelo shook his head. "I didn't do anything to you. That was all Dante. Please, I just want to leave. Can you let me do that?"

"No."

Angelo contemplated for just a moment about how he was going to get out of this situation alive. Elena was unstable at the moment, having already killed Dante. He didn't want to be next. There was only one thing that he could think of that she might agree to. It was worth a shot. The alternative was unthinkable.

"He's gone, you took care of him. He can never hurt you again. It was in self defense, we all know that. But if you kill me, it won't be self defense. I'm not a threat to you. I have no weapons on me."

Her eyes travelled to the gun at his feet, and back up to his face. Still, she didn't speak.

"You don't want to kill two people tonight, do you?"

Elena didn't move a muscle.

"Look, if you want, you can call the police and turn me in. I'll confess to taking the money. But please don't hurt me."

He meant every word of it. It wouldn't be the first time he would spend time in prison. And probably wouldn't be the last. He could do time standing on his head. It was better than dying.

"Ma'am, please. Just call the cops. I won't fight it."

And without another word, Elena pulled the trigger.

CHAPTER 17

"Elena!" Sergio howled as he ran from the living room. He had managed to get himself off of the couch while Angelo was pleading in the hallway with his wife.

Sergio was done waiting for orders, and didn't care if the man came back brandishing his gun. Though they could hear the conversation in the hallway, none of them could see the pair, so they didn't know who got shot. It was obvious that their stand-off was tense, but all feared that if they started yelling instructions to anyone, it would end in disaster. But it didn't matter.

Sergio rounded the corner of the hallway, tripping over the body of Angelo. Arms still tied behind his back, it took a moment to right himself. He locked eyes with his wife. She was unblinking.

Sergio took in her disheveled appearance, wide eyes, and blood stained clothing. He feared the worst had happened to her.

"Elena, honey, drop the gun."

Her hand released its death grip on the gun. It hit the

floor with a thunk, bouncing twice more before coming to a rest at her feet.

Sergio walked over to his wife. "Honey, are you all right?"

"Yeah." Her voice was barely above a whisper.

"Is he…are they both…dead?"

"Yeah."

He turned around, his tied arms facing her. "Can you get these off of me please?"

She nodded and walked into the kitchen. Sergio followed, not wanting to let her out of his sight. "We'll be right back," he told Tommy and Rosie.

They returned to the living room only seconds later, Elena holding a steak knife. Tommy and Rosie were already making their way to their feet. Sergio turned his back to his wife. In a flash, his zip ties fell to the floor.

Turning back around to face her, he reached for the knife. "Let me have that, okay?" He did his best to keep his voice light. He could see the fragile state she was in and didn't want to startle her. She nodded and handed him the knife.

Sergio wrapped his arms around his wife. He could feel her shuddering breaths against him. It broke his heart.

A moment later, he released her, and looked her in the eyes. They looked sad, and desperate. "I need to untie the others, okay?"

"What about your head? You're still bleeding."

Without thinking, he reached up and touched the side of his head. It was still pounding from the gun slamming into the side of it. Pulling back his hand, he saw just a bit of blood. "It's fine. Barely bleeding. I'll live."

"Serg, let me clean that up for you…"

Without responding to his wife, Sergio walked over and released his friends from their restraints. They had been conspicuously quiet during the entire scene playing out in front of them.

Tommy ran into the hallway and came back out a minute later. "She's right, they're both dead."

"We need to call the police," Rosie told them, as she walked toward the phone on the bar.

"No!" Elena's words stopped Rosie in her tracks. "I can't go to jail. Please, don't make me go to jail."

"No, honey," Rosie responded, "it was self-defense. You won't go to jail. And we have all this money sitting here, along with that open wall they bashed in. This will all prove why they were here."

"But I shot them...both of them. They are dead because of...me," Elena said, barely able to get the words out. A single tear dribbled its way down her cheek.

"No one is going to blame you," Tommy told her. "We are all witnesses. We'll make them understand that it was self-defense. I think with all of this evidence they wouldn't be able to think otherwise. You understand that, right?"

"But you weren't in the bedroom." Elena looked over at her husband. "You don't know what happened in there."

Sergio balled his fists, not even realizing it until he felt his nails dig into his palms. He looked down at his hands and relaxed them.

He walked up to his wife, and leaned in to whisper. "Do you want to tell me what happened? We can go outside to talk, if you prefer."

"No, no, it's okay," she said loud enough for everyone to hear. "He didn't...didn't...um...assault me."

Sergio let out a breath of relief.

"He tried, but I was able to hit him over the head with that bear statue on the nightstand. It was pretty heavy. He stopped when I did that."

"Then what happened?" Tommy asked.

Elena looked over at Tommy, but she almost didn't register him standing there. Her eyes were dead.

Rosie walked over and put her hand on Elena's back, gently rubbing it in an attempt at helping her friend relax a bit. She had been through a horrific ordeal. Rosie couldn't even imagine how Elena was feeling at the moment. She could feel Elena's back tensing up at her touch, so she removed her hand.

"It's okay, honey. You don't have to talk about it right now, if you don't want to." Rosie gave her husband a look. He averted his eyes.

"Let me get you some water. Sit down, I'll be right back," she told Elena.

CHAPTER 18

When Rosie returned from the kitchen, she handed the water to Elena, who drank it greedily. Passing the glass back to her friend, Elena thanked her. "I didn't realize how thirsty I was."

"Do you want to go change your clothes?" Rosie asked. "We can put these in a bag for the police."

"I don't want to call the police. He didn't assault me. So I have no proof of what happened here," Elena tried to explain.

"He did assault you though. Maybe not in the way you are talking about, but you were assaulted. You have scratches and bruises and bloody clothing to prove it. Besides, you don't need proof. Like I said, we are witnesses. The cops will take one look and will believe you, I can promise you that," Rosie explained.

"You can't promise me that," Elena told her.

"Okay, okay," Tommy interrupted. "We need to figure out what to do. I vote for dumping the bodies and keeping the money."

All three turned to look at him, not believing what had just come out of his mouth.

"Are you serious right now?" Rosie asked him. "We can go

to prison for probably a dozen charges related to what you just said."

"Who's gonna turn us in? You?" he asked his wife. She just stared at him. "You?" he asked Sergio.

"Not me," Sergio replied, with a shake of his head.

"And I know Elena won't," Tommy added. "So you are the only hold out, my dear."

Rosie threw up her arms. "I can't do this right now."

She turned to Elena. "Come on, let's get you changed. You can use the other bedroom."

She took Elena by the shoulders and guided her toward the loft bedroom.

While the wives were gone, Sergio and Tommy discussed what to do.

"I want to explain. Hear me out," Tommy tells his friend. "What if we just keep the money, like I said? We could split it."

"Split it?" Sergio asked.

"Yeah, fifty-fifty. No one needs to know about it."

"But there's one little problem." Sergio cocked his head toward the hallway. "Two big problems, actually."

Tommy shrugged and looked toward the living room window. "We are in a huge forest. If a couple of thieves end up buried out there, who's gonna know?"

Sergio thought about it. "You do have kind of a point. How much money do you think is in those duffles?"

"Hard to say, but I'd guess a couple mill," Tommy told him.

"We could really use that money," Sergio told him. "Business has been slow lately."

"Same." Tommy looked around the room. "We could pay off this cabin and maybe even buy a couple more."

"Sooo, back to our friends in there," Sergio said. "We should probably have a conversation with the wives before we make any decisions, don't you think? They are going to have to live with the consequences too. From the sound of it, your wife might be a hard sell on digging holes in the forest. And this is a lot of money to deal with. We…"

"We need to turn the money over to the cops." Both men turned to see Rosie and Elena walk back in. "No way we are keeping it," Rosie added.

Elena hadn't said anything. She had changed her clothes, washed her face, and brushed her hair. She looked much improved from a half hour prior. But the sadness in her eyes was palpable.

Sergio made a beeline for her and wrapped his arms around her once more. His heart was breaking for what his wife had gone through. Though Dante hadn't been successful in what he set out to do, as Sergio feared he might at the time, she had killed two men. Self-defense or not, it had to be traumatic for her.

Tommy and Rosie witnessed the moment between them. They could almost feel the heart wrenching pain that the pair was feeling.

A few minutes later, Sergio turned back to the couple. "So what do we do now?"

"We are not calling the cops," Tommy told the group bluntly.

"The hell we aren't," Rosie responded to her husband.

All three turned to Rosie. "You all are out of your minds. I need a minute."

They watched her walk to the kitchen, closing the door behind her.

"Do you think she'll come around?" Sergio asked Tommy, with raised eyebrows.

Tommy let out a cleansing breath. "God, I hope so. But she can be unpredictable at times. I just don't have any idea where she's going to land on this one."

In the kitchen, Rosie grabbed the corkscrew and opened the bottle of wine that she had left on the counter earlier that evening. Pulling a glass from the cupboard, she poured herself a generous helping.

She leaned back against the counter top as she sipped the wine. *What the hell are we going to do?*

She let her mind wander over the possible outcomes of this whole night:

One. They call the cops and all get arrested. No, she didn't really think that it would play out like that.

Two. They call the cops, who will take one look at the scene, and believe all of them. This seems the most likely, but could it really happen just like that? So easy with no problems? She shrugged.

Three. They hide the money, then call the cops about a break-in. But the cops might wonder why there is a wall in the living room missing most of its drywall. That might be tough to explain, especially with two dead bodies lying about.

Four. They bury the bodies and keep the money. Patch the drywall, get rid of all the evidence, and go on with their lives. Hmmm, would that really work? If they could all keep their mouths shut, it might be the most reasonable thing to do. At least they wouldn't be spending the foreseeable future in prison.

Could they make that work? Were they all trustworthy enough to never say a word to a single soul, for the rest of their lives? They would have to trust each other completely. It's the only way this would work.

Then there was Elena. She was the wild card in this whole plan. Sure, she was the one who didn't want to call the police, but that doesn't mean she can keep her cool about it permanently. Ugh, this whole thing got out of hand quickly.

Rosie gulped the rest of her wine and set the glass on the

counter. When she entered the living room, they were all staring at her.

"What?"

Tommy walked over to her. "What's going on with you darling? We are all worried about you."

Rosie shrugged. "I'm fine. At least as fine as I can be under the current circumstances."

"So…" Tommy began, "we've been talking while you were in the kitchen, doing whatever it was that you were doing. We think we should get rid of the bodies, split the money, get the wall repaired, and never speak of it again. Do you think you can get on board with that?"

"I'm not touching those bodies." Rosie crossed her arms in front of her chest.

"I can't…I just…can't," Elena told her. "Please don't make me."

"Oh honey, no one expects you to go near them. Don't worry about that," Rosie told her gently. "No matter what, we will take care of it. You don't have to worry about a thing."

CHAPTER 19

"Honey, look," Tommy said directly to his wife, "if we call the cops, they will grill Elena here." They all turned to look at her. Elena's eyes grew big. "We don't want that. What is it going to accomplish anyway? They are already dead, so no one is going to jail. It's only going to traumatize her further."

Rosie turned to her friend. "What do you want? Really think about it. Are you up for this or should we just get rid of these bodies and pretend it never happened? I think you should be the one to decide."

All eyes turned to Elena. Her cheeks flushed.

"I...I don't...want to talk to the cops," she replied. "I just... can't."

Standing next to her, Sergio wrapped his right arm around her waist and pulled her close to his side. She buried her face in his chest. "Then we won't call them. Tommy and I can take care of the bodies. Don't you worry about that."

"What about the money?" Rosie asked. "That's not ours."

"It could be," her husband replied, with a slight grin. "I mean, come on, we could really use the money, don't you think?"

"It's not ours, Tom."

"Then who does it belong to? Those guys?" He used his thumb to point in the direction of the back bedroom. "They certainly don't need it anymore. And no one knows it's here. So I don't see the problem with us keeping it."

"I don't know..." Rosie told him. "It just seems like a bad idea to me. I mean, did you all not see the movie 'A Simple Plan'? Remember how that went down?"

Tommy laughed. "Oh my dearest, this is not a Hollywood movie. This is real life. Besides, we are all good friends." He turned to Sergio and Elena. "Right?"

They both nodded.

"See? We would never turn on each other. All we need to do is put the money away for a while, make sure no one comes looking for it, and keep our big mouths shut." He turned back to the pair. "We can all do that, yes?"

They both nodded again. "Yes, we can definitely do that," Sergio added.

"Yeah, of course everyone is going to agree," Rosie responded. "That's because you all want millions of dollars. I guess I can't blame anyone for that. It's a lot of money. But I don't know. I just see future problems. For instance, what if more bad guys come looking for the money? Or worse, what if more bad guys come looking for those two dead ones in the back there?"

She looked over at Elena and quietly said she was sorry. Elena nodded.

"No one knows they are here." Sergio told her. "At least, I doubt anyone does. Who would send these two buffoons to do this job? They had to have decided on their own to do this. Which means, probably no one else knows."

"Probably?" Rosie asked. "Didn't they mention a boss earlier?"

Sergio shrugged. "Well, yeah, maybe they did. I don't

remember for sure. Unless they come back to life, and tell us what their plan was, there is no definitive way for us to know. So *probably* is the best I can do."

"Okay, but either way those two men had to have heard about the money from somewhere. And that means that others could have heard about it too." Rosie shook her head, and folded her arms across her chest. "I don't like it. I think it's a bad idea to keep the money. A really bad idea."

"Look, honey, I understand your reluctance," Tommy told his wife. "But none of that changes anything. If someone is going to come looking for the money, they would do that whether we keep it or not. So why not keep it?"

"I'm with Tommy here," Sergio chimed in. "Listen to him. What he's saying makes a lot of sense."

"Yeah," Tommy said. "We split the money fifty fifty, and never tell anyone. Not a soul. We just have to be careful about spending it. Like spend it slowly. And don't go make a one million dollar, or however much it is, deposit into your bank. That will certainly bring up serious red flags. Hide it somewhere and spend some here and there. Be nonchalant about it."

"Well you sound like you've been thinking about this a lot," Rosie teased him.

"I've seen those movies too where a group of people find a big wad of cash, like in a crashed plane or something. I think that's the one you were talking about. And then they screw everything up by spending it and turning on each other. So yeah, I know better," he smiled. "And that's the most important thing, we need to not say a word to anyone, and promise to never turn on each other. No matter what."

"Deal," Sergio said immediately.

They turned to Rosie. She hesitated.

"Tell you what," Tommy told her, "I'll call an alarm company first thing in the morning and order a state of the art alarm system for this place." He scanned the room. "Will that make you feel safer?"

She nodded. "That's a good idea."

"Sooooo.....?" Tommy looked at her with expectant eyes.

"Yeah, okay fine. I don't like it, but I'm outnumbered, so I guess I'm in."

All three looked at Elena. "Honey, you have to agree if we want to make this work," Sergio told her.

Elena didn't hesitate. "It's fine. I never did want to call the police, so I agree."

"Great," Tommy replied. "Tomorrow, Sergio and I can fix that drywall. But tonight we need a couple of shovels, 'cause we have them to deal with."

All eyes turned toward the hallway.

CHAPTER 20

"Silver Lake is just up the road." Tommy began digging through their linen closet for a couple of blankets to wrap the bodies in. "Instead of all the trouble of digging graves, why don't we just dump them in there?"

Sergio turned to him with a wide-eyed look. "Have you lost your mind? Bodies always turn up eventually when in water. They float up, swimmers find them, the water recedes due to drought, whatever, but they always turn up. Bad idea. If they are in the ground, it's way less likely anyone will ever find them."

Tommy stopped what he was doing. "You sound like you have experience in this department." He was only half kidding.

Sergio shrugged. "Nah, I just watch a lot of crime shows. Elena calls me her criminal in the making. I like to think that I am the detective in the making."

Tommy just nodded slightly. If the circumstances weren't what they were that night, they probably would have had a beer and a good laugh over that one.

"Yeah, I guess you are right, the water thing doesn't really make sense. Besides it's near my cabin. I don't want any investigators snooping around here when those bodies surface," Tommy told him.

He found two old quilts in the back of the linen closet. "Eureka! These will work." He showed them proudly to Sergio.

One was done in a log cabin quilt block, in colors of red, white and blue. The other was done in an eight pointed star block, in colors of brown, orange, and yellow. Tommy was pretty sure that Rosie's grandmother had made them. And normally, he wouldn't dare use them in the manner that they were about to use them, but he didn't really have much of a choice. They didn't have anything else that would work for wrapping and transport of bodies. Maybe she wouldn't miss them.

"Okay perfect, let's start with Angelo here in the hallway. We can get him out of the way," Sergio ordered.

"Don't you find it weird that we know their names?" Tommy asked, laying the blanket on the floor next to the dead body, and straightening it out the length of the man. "It seems to me that criminals would know better than to use their own names in front of their victims. But then again, maybe they are made up. We might never know."

Sergio stepped over the large man and knelt down, rolling him onto the blanket. "Nah, I think they are their real names. These two idiots didn't seem bright enough to come up with alternate names, and then remember to actually use them."

Tommy shrugged. "Maybe."

Once the body was rolled onto the blanket, Tommy wrapped each side over the top of him. "Okay, I think he's ready. You grab that end, and I'll get this one," he said as he made his way to the man's feet. "Let's get him out back and then we can go and get his partner in there." Tommy tilted his head toward the bedroom at the end of the hall.

Twenty minutes later, both bodies were outside the back door. Tommy went back into the kitchen to grab a couple of flashlights.

"Rosie, honey, we are going to go dig some holes now. It might take us a while."

"Okay, I'll start working on the blood clean up in here. I think we have a jug of bleach under the sink. Elena is resting in the loft. I can take care of this by myself."

"Lock the doors behind us," he called as the door slammed behind him.

Once outside, shovels in hand, Tommy spoke first. "How are we going to get both bodies and two shovels way out there in the forest? Three trips, I guess?"

"Do you have a wheelbarrow? Or two?"

"You know, I don't know the answer to that," Tommy told him. "I haven't had the chance to really check out everything here, since we haven't lived here long. Let's check the shed. There's a lot of stuff in there that the previous owners left behind. We may have to dig around."

Five minutes later, they emerged from the shed with a wheelbarrow.

"I don't know if we can get both of them in here," Tommy told his friend. "But let's try and see if it'll work."

By the time they were done heaving the bodies into the wheelbarrow, the pair was covered in dirt and sweat. It didn't matter that it was probably forty degrees out. But they did manage to get the bodies in, tossing their guns down into a crevice between the men and the metal. Getting it across the forest floor was another problem altogether.

CHAPTER 21

"Good god, these two are heavy." Tommy grunted under the weight of the wheelbarrow he was pushing over the soft forest ground that had become spongy from the rain and snow. The clouds dragged over the top of the trees.

"I can take my turn now, if you want," Sergio offered, shuffling the two shovels under the opposite arm.

"Yeah thanks." Tommy set the wheelbarrow down. Sergio dropped the shovels and took over.

Once Tommy gathered the shovels, the men were on their way.

It took a good thirty minutes before they felt they were far enough from the cabin to start digging.

Sergio grabbed a shovel and started first. "Come on, let's get this over with. Dig as deep as you can. We don't want any animals to come dig these two creeps up."

A light misty rain fell on their heads, causing both men to look up. "Fuckin' wonderful," Sergio spewed out, louder than he really should have. "What else? Seriously, what else could possibly happen to make this night any worse?"

He wasn't really speaking to Tommy. It was more of a general question, out to the world, to the gods, to any creatures that might be within hearing range.

"Dude, shhh, keep your voice down?"

Sergio looked around. "Who do you think is out here in the wee hours of the morning, listening to me complain?"

Tommy shrugged. "Yeah, I'm sure there's no one. But we don't need to be making more noise than we need to, you know, just in case someone is out here camping or something."

"No one is out here camping. I can promise you that," Sergio told him.

Tommy rolled his eyes. But it was so dark that his annoyance went undetected. "Okay, okay, let's not argue. Let's just get this done. I want to get home, out of the cold, and back to my wife."

They laid both flashlights on the ground, pointing at the spot where they would be digging.

An hour later, they felt they had dug to a sufficient depth. The men were covered in sweat and were filthy. It was the middle of the night by then and it was getting quite chilly in the forest. Neither had thought to bring a jacket.

Together, they tipped the wheelbarrow just enough for the bodies to roll into the makeshift grave. The pair stood over them, looking in.

"Should we say something?" Tommy asked, without taking his eyes off of the entangled bodies below them.

Sergio gave him a look and shook his head slightly. "Yeah, I got something to say." He proceeded to spit on them. "That's for my wife, you assholes."

"Is that really a good idea?" Tommy asked. "Now your DNA is on them."

"We've been handling these two for hours. I think that ship has sailed," Sergio explained.

Tommy shrugged. "Throw the wheelbarrow in there too. I don't want that thing around my house now."

Once they were buried, and some pine needles, leaves, and rocks had been scattered over the grave, the pair felt that it looked natural enough. No one walking by would suspect there were bodies under their feet.

They found a ravine and threw the shovels in. With sweat dripping down the backs of both of them, the chill in the air made them shiver. The forest was quiet, and the air had thickened. The change in the weather was evident. Autumn rains had cooled the forest down.

The walk home was silent.

Rosie opened the door of the cabin when they finally made their way back. The sky was just beginning to lighten up, with hues of lavender and orange on the horizon.

Not caring about the mess that he was, she wrapped her arms around her husband. "I was starting to get worried. You two were gone for so long. Is it all...done?"

Both men nodded. "Yeah, it's done," Sergio told her.

"It took most of the night, but everything here is cleaned up," she explained. "It might not pass a Luminol test, but barring that, I think we're good."

"How is she doing?" Sergio tipped his head toward the loft bedroom that Elena was resting in.

"She's been out since you left," Rosie told them. "She'll probably be up soon."

"Okay, good. I think I'm going to take a shower, and see if I can do something about this gash on the side of my head."

"I think there are some of those butterfly bandage things in the drawer in the bathroom," Rosie told him.

"Perfect. Then we are just going to go home, once she's up and ready."

Tommy and Rosie understood. "Of course," Tommy replied. "And don't worry about the drywall, I can patch it up. Just take your wife home. She probably can't wait to get out of this place, and I don't blame her."

Sergio started to head toward the bathroom.

"Wait," Tommy called. "What do you want to do about the money? Should we split it up now, or leave it here to deal with another time?"

Sergio turned to look at him, and thought for a moment. "I think that if those two knew the money was here, there might be others. We should split it now, and not take the chance that someone else might come looking for it."

"Yep, good plan. We can start working on that while you two are getting ready."

CHAPTER 22

Tommy scanned the pile of money. "Rosie, honey, let's get started on this now. It's gonna take a while to count all this up."

When Sergio emerged from the bathroom, freshly showered with his head bandaged, the pair was hard at work splitting up the bundles containing ten thousand dollars each. He knelt down on the soft faux bearskin rug. "Okay, where are we?"

"We've got three hundred and seventy thousand dollars in each duffle bag so far," Tommy told him. "Why don't you start making piles of a hundred thousand each, and we'll keep count that way. Otherwise, we might get off track here."

"Will do," he responded. "Any stirrings from Elena up there?"

All three looked toward the loft. Rosie shook her head. "Not a peep. Poor thing must be exhausted. We have been trying to keep pretty quiet, for her sake."

Sergio nodded and began working on his task immediately.

An hour later, the money had been split evenly between

the two duffle bags. Just a tad over one million dollars each. Just as they zipped up the bags, Elena walked down the stairs.

Everyone turned to face her. "How are you doing, honey?" Rosie asked her.

Elena crossed her arms and scrunched her eyebrows together. "I'm fine. You can all stop asking me that now. That man didn't…you know. So I'm fine."

"Yeah, but you killed two people. That is what we are worried about," Rosie added.

"They deserved it."

"Even so, that can't be easy for you," Tommy told her.

"I told you, I'm fine, and won't lose any sleep over it." Elena was getting tired of her friends tiptoeing around her, even though it had only been a few hours. "Come on Serg, let's go. I want to go home."

Over the next few months, regardless of her words, Elena wasn't fine. The nightmares overtook her life. Lack of sleep, a short temper, and frequent fights with her husband ruled their world.

Sergio did his best to deal with it all, and he did understand that what she went through was quite traumatic for her, but it was all beginning to grate on his nerves. The couple found themselves almost constantly at odds.

Elena sought out the help of a therapist for her nightmares and short temper. She was told in no uncertain terms by Sergio that she cannot ever speak about the events that took place in the cabin.

"Yeah yeah, Serg, I know. I'm not stupid."

"I know, honey, I'm just trying to gently remind you. Even though therapists are not supposed to tell anyone about what goes on in therapy, it still sometimes happens. Especially if he finds out you killed two men."

Elena narrowed her eyes at her husband. He raised his palms toward her. "Sorry."

~

Tommy and Rosie were very careful, and only spent a bit of cash, here and there, as promised. They went out to dinner with it, and bought a few items for their house. Other than that, no one would even know they came into some money.

On the other hand, Sergio and Elena were spending money like it was falling out of the sky. They took a couple of lavish European vacations, and frequently paid for all of their growing group of friends' dinners and drinks. The therapist, who was way more expensive than Sergio cared for, was their most expensive cash purchase, as it went on for months. But she was the one Elena wanted to talk to. So he relented.

This new lifestyle of theirs was putting a serious dent in the duffle bag money.

Within a few months, their new-found fortune had dwindled down to under a hundred thousand dollars, and they were beginning to get nervous.

"How the hell did we go through so much money so fast?" Sergio asked, as he rummaged through the duffle bag, counting the money for the third time, just to be sure he got it right.

"That's easy," his wife replied. "Vacations, buying our friends dinner and drinks, and therapy, to name a few. And two brand new, expensive cars. Oh, and our kitchen and backyard remodels. We've been spending like there's no tomorrow. I told you we were running through it." She crossed her arms, trying not to sound too judgmental, since she enjoyed the rewards as much as he did.

Sergio dropped the stack of cash he had been holding, into the duffle bag and zipped it up. "Yeah."

"We need to slow our spending, don't you think?" Elena asked her husband.

"Yeah, I know. We do still have a nice chunk of change, but most of it is gone. I guess we had our fun though."

Elena smiled. "Yes we did. But let's try to cut back and save some of this. I still want to have a family one day, and that money will certainly come in handy."

"I wonder how Tommy and Rosie are doing with their money?" Sergio asked. "I haven't noticed anything new, really. Have you?" he asked his wife.

She shook her head. "No. They are being really frugal with it. I know for a fact that they haven't even spent fifty thousand of it. I'm starting to wish that we had been more careful. I mean, did we really need cars that cost over a hundred thou each?"

Sergio shrugged. "I like our cars. But I know what you mean." He turned to look her in the eyes. "Our biggest ongoing expense is that therapist of yours. At three hundred dollars a pop, she's cleaning us out."

Elena raised her voice. "No she's not. Are you blaming me for spending all of our money? I'm the one who was traumatized. I'm the one who had to kill two men, and probably saved all of our lives. Are you telling me this is my fault?"

He walked over to his wife and put his arms around her. "No, of course not. But can you scale back to just once a week with her? We are running out of money."

Elena pulled out of his embrace. "Screw you."

She ran to their bedroom, slamming the door and locking it behind her.

CHAPTER 23

The still darkness of the forest at two a.m. was unnerving. The clouds seemed to slither through the tall pines and cedars surrounding him. A distant howl. A screech nearby. Each time he jumped, once dropping the shovel.

"Dammit!"

He glared at the forest, as if that would help. It didn't.

Sweat drizzled down his forehead and into his eyes. Every time, he pulled off a dirty glove and wiped it away with his bare hand, then swiping it on his pant leg.

Only once did he attempt to wipe the sweat with the dirty glove. He learned not to do that the hard way. It took almost a full bottle of water to wash the debris from his corneas. The words he yelled into the night echoed off of faraway rocks. Only the night creatures heard them.

He cursed the moonless night as he worked on his task. It was both a blessing and a curse. Sure, no one would be able to see him, but that was also his problem. He could barely see what he was doing. He had thought to bring a flashlight, but it was weak. The batteries must be getting low, he thought. Just perfect. And while he dug, the flashlight was on the ground, its dim glow not much help at all in pushing back the impeding darkness.

It took exactly one hour and twelve minutes for him to find what he was looking for in the packed forest floor.

"Bingo."

He dropped the shovel and picked up the flashlight, sticking the end of it in his mouth. He retrieved the gun from the hole in the ground, turning it over and over in his hands, wiping away as much dirt as possible while still wearing his dirty gloves. It was important that he didn't touch the gun directly. Fingerprints weren't much of a problem to wipe away, but he wasn't sure how difficult it was to clean all of his DNA from it, and didn't want to take any chances.

Better to be safe and keep the gloves on for now.

He checked the chamber and found that it still had three bullets in it.

"Excellent," he mumbled, the flashlight still in his mouth. He grabbed it and laid it back on the ground, pointing at the makeshift grave.

Not wanting to call attention to the two bodies lying in front of him, he tossed the gun to the ground a few feet to his side, and grabbed the shovel once again.

It was no longer necessary to be careful with his work. The gun was safely obtained. Now he just needed to get the dirt back onto those bodies, and be done with them. Permanently.

The task of re-burying them took twenty minutes, tops. He walked over their graves and stomped the dirt in tightly, then packed a few more shovels of dirt over the top of them. Gathering up enough leaves, pine needles, and other forest debris, to effectively cover his work, took a few more minutes.

He stood back, eyeing the area in front of him. It looked good. No one would have a clue that the bodies of two degenerates were only inches below their feet. He only needed to worry about hungry animals. But there was nothing he could do about that.

He shrugged. "It'll have to do."

The man picked up the shovel one last time and flung it as hard as he could into the void of the forest.

Gun safely stowed in his jacket pocket, the man began the trek toward his next destination.

CHAPTER 24

The pounding on the kitchen door of the cabin startled Tommy and Rosie, who were sound asleep.

"What the hell?" Tommy grumbled out as his feet touched the cold wooden floor of their bedroom. "You expecting someone?"

She turned to the clock radio on her nightstand and squinted at the red glowing numbers. "Who would I be expecting at four twenty-five a.m.?"

Rosie also climbed out of bed and shrugged into her thick purple robe. She loved the warmth and feel of the soft furry material. Bending over, she fished her socks from the floor and put them on. Tommy, wearing nothing but pajama bottoms, was already out of the bedroom by the time she was ready.

Rosie flipped on the light in the hallway as she walked toward the pounding noise. It was coming from the kitchen door, which was very odd. Why would someone go to their kitchen door instead of the front door?

She watched as Tommy pulled the yellow curtain with

daisies on it to the side. He pulled open the door without hesitation.

"What the hell are you doing here in the middle of the night?" Tommy asked.

"I need to talk to you." He looked over at Rosie, with her hair sticking up in all directions. "Both of you. Sorry to wake you."

"What is this all about?" Tommy asked.

"I'll make some coffee." Rosie turned toward the coffee pot and began filling it with water. "Hon, you want some? Sergio, how about you?"

Both men nodded.

"Come sit down." Tommy indicated the kitchen table with a flick of his hand. His naturally blond hair formed an almost perfect mohawk during his sleep. He ran his finger through it as he sat down.

Sergio sat in the chair across from him.

"Why are you covered in dirt?" Tommy asked him, eyeing the man from head to toe.

"Don't worry about it." Sergio's voice was gruff and irritable.

Rosie thought she would try to ease the thick tension hanging in the room. "What's going on, Serg? It must be serious, since you are here at this ungodly hour." She glanced out into the darkness of the night. It would be another hour before the sun would begin to peek over the hills.

The men watched Rosie as she carefully poured three mugs of coffee and carried theirs over, setting them down in front of each man, before returning for hers. Once she was seated at the table, she and Tommy looked to Sergio for answers.

"Well?" Tommy prompted. "Are you going to tell us what is going on or not?"

"Is Elena okay?" Rosie asked.

Sergio turned to her. "She's fine. She's the reason I am here."

The thing was that Elena had no idea he was there. He had stealthily creeped out of the house once she had fallen asleep and he felt she was truly deeply out for the remainder of the night. He could get his task done and be back before she realized he was even gone.

"What do you mean?" Rosie asked. "Why isn't she here with you?"

"Because she doesn't know I'm here."

"Are you going to tell us why you are here or not?" The tone of Tommy's voice made it perfectly clear that he was losing patience with the whole ordeal.

"Yeah, I'm going to tell you. I...we...need money," Sergio blurted out.

The couple looked at each other. "What do you mean, you need money?" Rosie asked. "You got a duffle bag with a million dollars in it a few months ago. Don't tell us that you spent it all already. Have you been gambling?"

Sergio looked her in the eyes. "It's not all gone, but most of it. As you know, Elena has been going to therapy over everything that happened. That's not cheap."

"I'm sure it isn't," Rosie replied. "But there's no way it cost anything near a million dollars. What is really going on?"

While the two of them talked, Tommy sat in silence. No one noticed his fists turning white.

Sergio looked at the cup of coffee in front of him, not wanting to meet their eyes. "And yes, I've also done some gambling. Most of the money is gone."

"What the hell, Sergio?" Tommy finally spoke up. "None of that is our fault or our problem. We split that money fifty-fifty. Just because we were careful with ours, doesn't give you any rights to it."

"We need the money," Sergio replied. "It won't be long

until we can't even pay our mortgage anymore. Just half, that's all I'm asking for. It will go a long way to getting us solvent again."

"No," Tommy said softly.

Rosie and Sergio looked at him. "Honey, maybe we can give them a little? I mean, with Elena's trauma and all, I don't mind helping them some," Rosie explained. "I didn't even want the money in the first place, so it's no problem for me."

Tommy was grumpy and tired from being awakened in the wee hours of the morning for this nonsense. He stood abruptly, bumping into the kitchen table and causing the mugs to rock. The coffee sloshed over the side. No one seemed to notice.

"I said no. We aren't giving you any money. That's ours, fair and square, and you know it. You got your share, and it's not our problem that you squandered it. Now leave us alone. I want to get back to bed." Tommy was not mincing words.

Sergio didn't want to do it, but felt that he had no choice. He reached into his jacket pocket and pulled out the dusty gun he had dug up a couple of hours prior.

He was prepared, knowing that it might come to this. He needed the money, and they were going to give it to him. No matter what.

Rosie gasped, as her hands flew up covering her mouth. She scooted her chair backward, away from the table, as if that would help if a bullet headed her way.

"I'm not asking," Sergio told them.

CHAPTER 25

Staring at the gun pointed straight at him, "You're kidding me, right?" Tommy replied. "I don't believe for even a second that you would use that gun on us. Where did you get that thing anyway? It looks like you dug it up from..." Tommy locked eyes with Sergio. "Oh no. Tell me you didn't."

"Yep, I dug it up from right where you and I left it."

He looked over at Rosie. Her face had turned an ashen gray. Tommy might have been smug enough to think there was no way Sergio would use the gun on them, but Rosie wasn't so sure about that.

To Rosie, Sergio had always had some rough edges around him. He was quick to snap at his wife, or anyone for that matter. He seemed to want to be in charge all the time. Rosie didn't really see what appeal Sergio had for Elena, but it wasn't her business. Their marriage was of no concern to anyone but them.

Regardless of what Tommy was saying, she knew he was somewhat intimidated by Sergio. In fact, Tommy was the one who suggested that they cut all ties with the Riveras after everything that had happened.

Rosie didn't want to do that though. Elena was her best friend. And she had gone through a lot. The attack. The shooting of both of those horrible men. Months of therapy afterward. No, Rosie couldn't just abandon her friend like that. It wouldn't be right, and it wouldn't be something that Rosie felt comfortable doing.

Now, standing in their cabin kitchen, she desperately wished that she had listened to her husband and dropped all contact with them. Not that it really would have mattered. Sergio knew where they lived. Them not being in contact could not have changed that fact.

"Where is the money?" Sergio asked, looking at the two frightened faces before him.

"We aren't telling you," Tommy answered. "You got your money, and what you did or did not do with it, is not our problem. This is our money, and if you ever try to strong arm us again, I'll call the police and tell them everything. They will know that your wife is the one and only person who killed both of those men. I'll make sure they even know that one of them was unarmed and pleading for his life."

Tommy folded his arms in front of him in defiance, doing his best to sound unintimidated by Sergio and his gun. He thought that being strong in his conviction would get Sergio to back down. They were friends. No matter what the man said, Tommy couldn't imagine him actually using the gun on them.

Sergio took a deep breath. "Don't you dare threaten me. And if you don't show me where that money is right now, you won't ever get the chance to talk with the cops. Got it?" He narrowed his eyes, hoping it was enough to get his point across.

"Honey, just tell him where it is. We can always make more money. It isn't worth all of this." Rosie couldn't say exactly what she was thinking, that it wasn't worth him killing them over.

She didn't really like having the money anyway. It kind of seemed cursed to her. The horrible way they came about getting it, and now this. It was all more than she could take.

Sergio pointed the gun right between Rosie's eyes. "Tell me now, or else."

Rosie's face drained of all blood.

Tommy's hands flew into the air in front of him, palms facing the man with the gun. "Okay, okay, I'll tell you. Please just leave her out of it."

Tommy's whole world revolved around his wife. He couldn't imagine for even a second, living without her. If it meant giving this man every last dime they had, then so be it. None of that mattered. Only Rosie mattered. If she were killed, it would be a devastation to him so profound that he knew he would never recover. Not ever.

"So, where is it?"

"It's...it's...outside under the back deck, in the crawl space," Tommy answered, his words were unsteady.

Sergio flicked the gun in the direction of the back door. "Let's go." He turned to Rosie. "All of us."

She nodded, thankful that the gun was no longer pointed right at her brain.

Tommy led the way out the door, with Rosie close behind him. She placed her hands on his back, so that Tommy knew she was there, but mostly to comfort the both of them. She was terrified, as was Tommy. Neither knew if they would survive the night.

Carefully stepping down the rough, uneven steps, Tommy led them to the door under their wooden deck. He had no shirt or socks on, and shivered in the early morning chill. Even in the autumn, it got pretty chilly at night in the mountains. Tommy put the cold out of his mind, even as he saw

Rosie pull her robe tightly in front of her and rub her arms to stay warm.

Tommy pointed. "It's in there. Most of it anyway."

"Most of it?" Sergio questioned.

"Yeah, it's been several months, we spent some of it. A few thousand is all, really. Most of it is still there."

It hurt Tommy down to his core to just hand over all that money to Sergio, a man who used to be a pretty good friend. That was all over the moment the man stepped into their house that early morning.

But if Sergio was serious about getting the money, or killing them for it, then Tommy would just have to live with handing it over. If they were dead, that money wasn't going to be any good to them anyway.

"Well aren't you two the poster children of restraint?" He grinned as he said it. "Lucky for us that you were. Now Elena and I get the rewards of that restraint. So, thank you."

Tommy didn't respond to the man's obvious taunting.

Sergio waved the gun at Tommy again. "Go get it. And don't try to pull anything. Rosie is staying here with me, and I won't hesitate to use this thing."

Rosie didn't say a word, but her eyes widened as she looked at the gun pointing her way, and back up into the face of the man who used to be their friend.

CHAPTER 26

Tommy stooped under the deck, doing his best to ignore the spider webs and the insects that clung to them. He hated spiders with a passion. It was all he could do to not think about them on his bare skin as he opened the door that was only four feet tall and ducked into the crawl space under the house.

He hadn't bother to lock the door when he hid the duffle bag with a million dollars in it under the house. Stupid? Probably. But they were kind of in the middle of nowhere. It was quite unlikely that anyone would come across their cabin by accident. And even if they did, it wouldn't dawn on anyone to go exploring down in the crawlspace. If they wanted valuables, they would go inside the cabin, not down in the creepy, dark dungeon below it.

It didn't take long before he realized that he hadn't grabbed a flashlight on his way out the back door.

"Hurry up! I don't have all day," Sergio called from above.

Tommy turned and stuck his head out the door. "It's extremely dark down here. Can you send Rosie inside to get the flashlight? It's in the kitchen drawer next to the fridge."

Sergio glanced over at Rosie, her eyebrows were high, in anticipation. He considered the request. He knew that if he allowed her to go inside, he was running the very real possibility that she would either run, or grab her cell and call the cops. Neither were a good choice.

On the other hand, if he followed her in, then Tommy was loose. He could run. Would he though? Sergio wondered. Would Tommy take off, knowing that he was leaving his very vulnerable wife there with a gun wielding thief? Sergio didn't think of himself as a criminal. He just needed to get that money. Money that Tommy and Rosie didn't technically have any right to in the first place.

Hell, they didn't even know it was in their walls when they bought the house. If those two men hadn't shown up to relieve them of the burden of so much money in their cabin, they likely would never have known it was there. So no, Tommy and Rosie didn't really have rights to it. It was completely up for grabs, as far as Sergio was concerned.

"No, she's not going anywhere. Do you think I'm an idiot?" Sergio asked. "Just find the damn money. You know where you put it, so it can't be that hard." He looked around at the dark just beginning to lift around them. "And hurry up about it. The sun will be up soon."

Tommy was having a hell of a time finding the duffle bag. He could have sworn that he left it in the far back left corner. It was pitch black and he was on his knees crawling around on the freezing dirt, searching for that corner. He had lost all sense of direction and had no earthly idea where he was under the house.

Oh, he found a corner. He sat back, with his head tilted under the floor of the kitchen above, and felt around in the area. Nothing but spider webs that made him flinch every time he encountered one. He reached all the way into the corner, and still nothing. He came to the conclusion that he was in the wrong corner.

So it must be to the left of me. I hope. He got back onto his hands and knees and crawled in the general direction of where he figured the far back left corner must now be.

He couldn't see his hands and feet, but knew instinctively that they were turning blue. He was losing feeling in all four extremities.

Blinding pain hit him squarely in the forehead.

Rosie jumped when Tommy yelled, "Ow! damn! That fucking hurt."

He stopped and pressed his right hand to his forehead. It didn't feel like there was blood. A giant bruise would not be unexpected.

He surmised he had run into a beam, that he didn't expect to be so low. His eyes were beginning to adjust to the darkness, and he could now make out some light and dark shapes. He looked above his head. *Yep, a beam.*

"You okay, honey?" Rosie called into the dungeon from above.

"Don't talk to him," Sergio ordered. "He needs to concentrate."

Rosie narrowed her eyes at the man with the gun. "He's trying. But it's pitch black down there and he's barefoot. What do you expect?"

Sergio turned the gun and pointed it directly at her midsection. "I don't appreciate your mouth. If you expect to survive this, then I suggest you shut it."

Her eyes widened at the sight of the gun pointing at her, and she moved a step to her left, to get out of direct fire. She didn't figure it would work, but what did she have to lose?

Sergio dropped his gun to his side, and looked her directly in the eyes. "Look, I don't want to kill you two. I wish it wasn't like this. I actually liked you."

"Then don't. Don't kill us."

Sergio averted his eyes.

Tommy resumed crawling in the same general direction. This time ducking under the beams that he could just make out in the darkness. He could feel something crawling on his back, and it took every bit of concentration he had to shake it off and keep moving. Their lives were at stake.

"Where is Elena? Does she know what you are here doing?" Rosie prodded.

Ignoring her, Sergio turned his attention back to the crawl space. "I said hurry up! What is taking so damn long?"

"Yeah, that's what I thought," Rosie added. "She doesn't know a thing about any of this, does she?" Not expecting an actual answer, she continued. "She has no idea you are here threatening us and stealing our fair share of the money. Am I right?"

"Tommy!" Sergio yelled. "I'm gonna shoot this bitch if you don't get up here with that money in the next thirty seconds!"

Rosie's eyes went wide and her mouth hung open. She took a step back from Sergio. She hadn't really thought Sergio was actually capable of shooting them. He just wanted the money, then would be on his way.

Now, she wasn't so sure. He had always been a bit aloof around them, but generally a nice guy. She was shocked at his outburst. *Come on Tommy, come on. Don't leave me here with the maniac.* The words rumbled around in her head.

"Here it is. Found it!" The voice came from somewhere deep under the house.

Rosie let out an audible breath of relief. It wasn't lost on Sergio. He didn't care. She was the least of his problems. He was about to get the rest of the money. Then what? He hadn't really thought the rest of the plan through.

CHAPTER 27

Sergio stifled the urge to pump his fist. Instead, he barked more orders. "Good, get up here. It's freezing, and I'm tired of standing out here. It has been a long night."

The duffle bag emerged before Tommy did, as he heaved it out the door first. When he reached it, and was able to stand, though hunched over under the deck, he grabbed the bag by the handles and dragged it behind him. He walked right into a spider web and squealed. If the situation hadn't been so dire, Rosie would have laughed at how ridiculous he was. But she couldn't, and wouldn't, muster any humor in the situation.

Once out from under the deck, Tommy stood, and flung the duffle bag in Sergio's direction. He looked down as it landed at his feet.

"Well, pick it up. We aren't leaving it out here for someone to grab." Sergio indicated the bag with a flick of his gun.

Tommy looked around. "Who's going to grab it? The nearest neighbor is probably a half mile away."

"Just do what I said, and get inside."

"Yeah, yeah, fine." Tommy picked up the bag. He and Rosie led the way back into the cabin.

Tommy dropped the bag on the living room floor. "Now can you just leave? We would like to go back to bed and forget this whole ordeal ever happened? I'm freezing and need a hot shower first."

Sergio laughed, despite his resolve not to. "Is that what you think is going to happen here? I'm just going to take the money, go home, and everyone is going to live happily ever after?"

"What do you mean?" Rosie dared to ask. She had a sinking feeling that things were about to get worse. Much worse.

He turned to look at her. *It's a shame she has to die. She really is a nice person.*

"I mean, that I have no choice but to kill the two of you."

Rosie gasped. "Why? We gave you what you wanted. You have the money. No one needs to know anything about it. You can have it. We don't even want it anymore. Please, just take it and go. We aren't going to mention this night to anyone."

"You know I can't do that. I can't trust that you won't open your big mouths about the money, the killing of those two men, me digging up the gun, and coming here tonight. No, that's a lot of stuff to trust you to never tell anyone. I can't take the risk."

"Hey, man," Tommy interrupted, "we swear never to tell another living soul. Just let us go. We don't care about any of that anyway. I mean, it's been what, six months since those two men broke in here and were shot dead? We haven't said a word to anyone. And we never would. We could be found responsible too. We don't want that. So, you can trust us."

Sergio considered what Tommy had just said. Sure, he was probably telling the truth. Sergio was sure that Tommy meant every word. But all he needed was for one little slip, five, ten, twenty years from now, and all hell would break loose. Elena could go to prison for killing those men, and he couldn't let that happen. No, he couldn't trust them to keep silent for the rest of their lives.

There was just too much at stake.

Sergio knew that if he thought about it too much, he could lose his nerve. Tommy was the bigger threat. That was obvious. He had to go first. Without another moment of hesitation, he pulled the trigger.

Rosie screamed as Tommy clutched his mid-section and went to his knees. She ran over to her husband, ignoring the real possibility that Sergio would probably shoot her before she reached him.

"Oh my god! Tommy! Oh my god!" She watched the blood squeezing between her husband's fingers and dripping onto the floor in front of him. Rosie turned to Sergio. "What have you done? You didn't have to do this."

Sergio didn't respond.

"I'm going to get you a towel," she whispered to her husband.

"Don't move."

Rosie turned to Sergio. "He's going to bleed to death if we don't do something."

"That's kind of the point."

Rosie's mouth fell open. "How can you be so callous? It's just money. We don't care about it. You can have it. Please, let me do something. Let me call an ambulance. You can leave. I'll tell them someone broke in."

"You think the cops are going to believe that you had two break-ins within six months? They aren't stupid, you know. Not completely anyway. They won't believe you. Then you will point them in my direction. See how that leaves me no choice here?"

"Sergio, please. We won't say anything. And the police don't know about the first break-in, so they won't put that together with this."

Sergio shook his head in silence.

"I don't know how else to get any of that across to you. We don't want to die." She glanced over at the duffle bag a few feet away. "That money means nothing to us. We don't even want it anymore. Just take it and go. Please, Tommy is dying. I need to help him."

Sergio didn't know why he was even still there, debating with Rosie. Maybe because they had all been friends once. He had truly liked Tommy before everything that happened that fateful night a few months prior.

Maybe because Elena and Rosie were best friends. He knew that the death of her friend would devastate Elena, and that is the only thing that gave him pause.

Rosie saw the blood draining from Tommy's face. He was getting paler by the minute. He could no longer stay upright on his knees and fell with a sickening thud to the wooden floor.

"Tommy!" Rosie knelt at his side. "Can you hear me?"

"Yeah." His words were weak…barely perceptible.

"Oh my god. He's dying. Hang on honey, I'm getting help."

Rosie stood, the gun pointing at her be damned. She took two steps toward the kitchen when the sound of the gun reverberated off the walls of the small cabin.

CHAPTER 28

The gunshot rang in Rosie's ears, and she stopped walking. For a moment, she wasn't entirely sure what had just happened. Then it hit her. The agonizing, searing pain in her gut. Looking down, she saw her blood stained pajama top. The crimson was spreading out, soaking her pajamas, as well as the purple robe she was still wearing.

She placed both hands over the wound. "Oh my god, you actually shot me. What the hell? I'm no threat to you."

She looked Sergio in the eyes as she pressed as hard as she could on the wound. The pain was almost unbearable, but she did everything she could to stay on her feet. If she went down, she knew that she would never get back up.

"Why did you do this?" she asked, indicating her mid-section. "Why cause this suffering? Why not just shoot us both in the head and be done with it?" Her words tumbled out as she asked each question in rapid succession without waiting for answers she knew would never come.

Sergio thought about those questions for a moment. "Probably because shooting you in the head seems so...so... final, I guess."

"And this isn't? Without help, we are going to die. It'll just be slow and painful. Is that what you want? To punish us for something? To make us suffer? I don't understand why you are doing any of this. We were telling the god's honest truth when we said that we would never tell anyone about any of this."

She glanced over at Tommy, who was very pale. And very still. She feared that she would never again get to hear him tell her that he loved her. Tears flowed down her cheeks.

"And if you call an ambulance, we still won't say a word," she added.

She looked at Tommy, praying for some sign of life from him...anything, anything at all. Just a tiny inhale of breath even, or a flick of a finger. But it didn't matter. Her knees finally gave way, and she went to the ground.

She landed on her right side, facing her husband. She looked up into Tommy's eyes, hoping for some sort of recognition from him. But his eyes were not looking back at her. They were fixed on something in the distance that she couldn't see. His face was almost pure white.

A stray beam of sunlight came in through the living room window, peeking between the curtains, landing squarely on Tommy's cheek. Regardless of what was happening at that very moment, the slightest of smiles formed in her eyes. Tommy had brought in that light, just for her.

Rosie's mind drifted to their wedding day. It was bright and sunny. The beach they were standing on had just the slightest hint of a breeze. Family and friends stood in front of them, beaming. It was the best day of their lives.

And this one was the worst.

"Tommy, honey, can you hear me?"

She knew at that moment that he would not...could not...answer her. He would never answer her again.

"Oh god, what have you done?" Rosie wailed. The sound

of her voice was almost primal. She had never felt such pain in her life. Not the pain in her stomach. The pain in her heart.

"Just do it now." She couldn't face another moment without the love of her life. "Just kill me and get it over with. I don't want to be here without him."

Rosie wanted nothing more than to shut her eyes. She didn't want to see what was coming next. But, for some reason, she couldn't will herself to close them. She wanted Sergio to know that he hadn't defeated them. The defiance in her face came through loud and clear.

Once more, a gunshot rang out in the cabin that early morning.

CHAPTER 29

"It had to be done," Sergio said aloud.

Sergio felt no regret. Okay, maybe a little regret. He wasn't a complete monster.

He and Elena needed the money. The others didn't. It never should have been theirs anyway. He hated the fact that he had to split it with them. But after those two thugs who broke in were killed, and the money was left behind, that's how things turned out.

The only tiny bit of remorse that eked into his soul was that Elena would be hurt by all of this. She wouldn't know that he did it, but that didn't matter. He knew. Rosie had been her best friend. He would have to help her to somehow learn to live with the fact that she no longer had a best friend in her life. It would be tough for her, but she'd get through it.

Sergio didn't need to check Rosie's pulse. The final shot, that cut a smaller than expected hole right above her left eye, was enough to finish the job. Her eyes were open and fixed. She stared into nothingness.

He placed the gun on the coffee table next to him, grabbed the duffle bag, and walked out the back door, without even glancing behind him. He had parked down the dirt road aways, so as not to alert them of his presence when he arrived. Pulling the key fob out of his pocket, he clicked it, and the trunk popped open. He placed the key fob back in his pocket. Dropping the duffle bag at his feet, he pushed aside a shovel, and fished two full gas cans out of the trunk.

After setting the cans down, he lifted the spare tire cover and placed the duffle back in the empty spot. The spare tire, which he prayed he wouldn't need, was currently propped up against a wall inside his garage.

Sergio carefully closed the trunk, still wary that someone could be in the forest watching him, even at this early morning hour. There was a distant growl and Sergio's head snapped and scanned the nearby trees. Nothing. He smiled, despite the situation he had found himself in. "Stop being ridiculous," he said aloud.

Picking up the two full gas cans, he hadn't been absolutely sure how the night was going to end, but had a pretty good idea. He came prepared.

Had Tommy not argued with him about the money, Sergio thought that he might just take it and not do what he did. But that isn't what happened. So this was all Tommy's fault, as far as he was concerned.

At about sixty total pounds, Sergio lugged the heavy cans to the cabin. He set one down on the deck outside the kitchen door and walked inside. He stood over the bodies, with the can in his hands. They seemed so peaceful. No matter what their problems were, they no longer had a care in the world. He thought that might not be such a bad thing after all.

Beginning with Tommy, Sergio lifted the can and poured the pungent liquid the length of his body, from his head to his feet. He followed suit with Rosie. It was imperative that there was nothing left to discover on their bodies. He didn't need the hassle any of this getting back to him somehow.

The bedrooms were next, as he soaked the beds and carpet. This was followed by the living room, and finally, the kitchen. It took about ten minutes for him to soak the inside of the cabin really well with the gasoline.

Once out on the deck, he threw the empty can inside the still open kitchen door. He heard it bounce around a few times, before it went silent. Picking up the second can, he began his lap around the outside of the house, soaking the point where the cabin met the dirt, splashing it occasionally up the side of the walls. He poured the last of it on the wooden decks.

Finishing up, he tossed the second can on the back wooden deck, where he had started, and stood back to admire his handiwork.

It wasn't his intention to start a forest fire, but if that was the result, then so be it. At least if that happened, it would go a long way in covering up the details of his crime. He did notice that the cabin was surrounded by dirt for a lot of feet, fifty maybe, before one got to the tree line. Because of this, the fire might not get to the actual forest.

Oh, Sergio had no illusions that the bodies would never be found. These days the investigators had sophisticated equipment, he was sure of it. So yes, Tommy and Rosie would be found, even if just parts of them. It was his job to make that as difficult as possible, and an extremely hot burning fire should do the trick.

CHAPTER 30

Sergio reached into his left pants pocket and fished out a book of matches. The printing on the front read, *The Starla Inn*. He laughed out loud at how trashy he thought the name sounded. The odd thing was that the inn was an old historic building, built around the turn of the last century, and was a place where those with a bit of money stayed. It was one of those places that people went to just to stay at the inn. Many never ventured out of the place to see the sights of the area. They just wanted to experience the lore of the place.

He remembered how excited Elena had been when he surprised her with a trip. She hadn't known where they were going until they pulled into the parking lot. He smiled at remembering the look on her face when she finally realized that they were actually going to stay there for the weekend.

It was a magical weekend for the two of them, and one neither would ever forget. They had eaten lobster for dinner, and walked along the beach to view the sunset each evening.

Neither of them had ever smoked, but there was a glass bowl, reminiscent of the giant goldfish bowl he had as a child, sitting on the check-in desk. He had absent-mindedly fished one out and deposited it in his pocket. Once home, it laid forgotten in the junk drawer in their foyer.

Sergio had grabbed it on the way out of the house this evening.

Taking one last look at it with his flashlight, he ripped out a single match, closed the cover, and struck it against the course striking surface. For just a brief moment, it lit up his face, and then dimmed to just a bit of light around his hand. Sergio tossed the lit match onto the surface of the deck.

Sergio stood in the dirt, several feet from the deck and watched it catch fire. It took less than a minute for the entire deck and a portion of the cabin to erupt in huge flames.

He stood, mesmerized by the sight. It was beautiful. The bright orange, yellow, and purple flames dancing in front of him. It calmed him. His breathing slowed as he watched the entire house being consumed.

After a few minutes, he realized that he should get out of there. All he needed was some plane or early morning hunter seeing the flames and calling the authorities. He turned to leave.

Turning back one last time, he threw the matchbook that was still in his hand, into the flames of the deck.

CHAPTER 31

Sergio sat in his car and reconsidered arriving home with the money in tow. He tilted the rearview mirror toward him, and stared into his own eyes. His face was sallow, his eyes dull.

Was he a horrible person? I was something he wondered about. Sure, many could...and would...argue that he was just that. Anyone who could murder and burn the bodies of two friends, good friends by all accounts, was a deranged psychopath.

Yet, he didn't feel like a psychopath. He was just someone who had a goal. Tommy and Rosie were just in the way, that's all. He really didn't feel any ill will toward them. Shit happened. He couldn't be blamed for doing what he had to do to get that money. It should have been his after all. After what Elena went through, Tommy should have offered every last cent to the two of them in the first place. Did he? Nah. And that's why this night happened.

Now, what to do about the money?

Once the burned out cabin and bodies were discovered, the cops might show up at his place, since they were close friends. If that happened, the money might be found. He didn't trust putting it in a safe deposit box at the bank. He had always been leery of banks in general. So no, that wasn't an option.

He racked his brain for ideas. Then it hit him. The spot in the forest. Their spot. *Yes, that would be perfect*, he thought. Turning over the ignition, he drove down the long dirt road that led from Tommy's cabin to the main road, and turned right. A few miles later, he turned right once again, onto another dirt road. Three miles in, he found the spot.

A year earlier, he and Elena had been out exploring the forest. It was something she really liked to do. He could take it or leave it, but went along to make his wife happy.

On that particular day, she had packed them a nice picnic lunch and they came across an old abandoned camping area near the lake. It had a handful of picnic benches and stone fire rings still containing the remnants of long ago fires. Footprints, both of the human and canine kind, were peppered around the campsite, revealing the fact that the site wasn't completely abandoned. Others did wander through from time to time.

"This is perfect," Elena told him, her voice high with excitement, as she climbed out of the car the moment it was parked.

Sergio met up with her at the edge of the lake, and they watched a flock of ducks enjoying the early afternoon sunshine near the shore. The ducks paid no attention to the two of them, clearly having been a bit domesticated by frequent visitors to the lake.

After enjoying the simple picnic of sandwiches and potato salad, with a bottle of wine, they decided to explore the area a bit. There were some trails, which really were nothing more than well worn paths, all around the campsite.

When the paths allowed, they walked hand in hand.

Other times, Elena led the way, with Sergio happy to follow her lead.

"Ooh, Serg, look at this tree. Isn't it beautiful?"

She stopped in front of a large redwood tree, that had to be several hundred years old, by Sergio's inexperienced guess.

Elena reached out and caressed the rough bark. "Let's get a pic in front of it." She fished her phone out of the pocket of the khaki colored chinos she wore, and held it out in front of them as far as she could reach.

"We can't really see much of the tree at this angle. She dropped her arm to her side. "Here, let's move out a bit, so we can get more in the shot."

Sergio did as he was told.

"This will have to do, I guess. This thing is so freaking huge that we will be tiny little ants in the photo if we try to get the whole thing in there." She held out the phone once again. "Say cheese."

Elena checked the photo on her phone. "Oh, that's a keeper."

Over the next several months, the two of them frequented the campsite and always sat under that tree. Elena had called it "our spot." It had become their favorite place to just be together.

CHAPTER 32

The early morning orange and violet sky was speckled through the trees as Sergio parked and popped open the trunk of his car once again. He fished out the shovel, along with the duffle bag from under the spare tire cover, where he had placed it previously. The shovel was something he hadn't really planned on using, as he initially planned to just take the duffle bag home with him. But he had always kept one in his trunk, because a person never knew when one would come in handy.

He hiked to their 'spot' under the redwood tree, and dropped the items at the base of the trunk. Standing under its massive frame for a few minutes, memories of happy times with Elena at that very spot flooded his brain.

"Okay, enough of that," he muttered aloud.

Sergio bent over and retrieved the shovel. He walked behind the tree, and went about ten feet to a good sized boulder. "This should work."

He didn't want to bury it right at the spot where they usually sat and held hands. It felt wrong somehow.

He was thankful that he didn't have to dig the type of hole needed for an entire human body. This hole was quite small, just large enough to squeeze the duffle bag into. After covering it up, he found some smaller rocks and placed them on top. Then a few handfuls of forest debris to cap off the illusion, and voila! Perfect, he thought. No one will have a clue.

On the drive home, Sergio was both excited and nervous. His hands shook as he tightened his grip on the steering wheel, having finally ditched those stupid gloves he had been wearing. They were somewhere off in the forest, after he flung them far and wide.

He was going to have to come clean with Elena. There was no way to sufficiently explain how he just happened to get all the money from Tommy and Elena on the very night that they were killed, without telling her the truth. He knew it wouldn't be long before the bodies were discovered. A cabin on fire was not easily overlooked.

It was after 7 a.m. when he finally pulled into the driveway of their modest two story house in their middle class neighborhood. Sergio owned his own business as a consultant for small business owners. It paid pretty well, but they weren't rich. Elena still did some modeling work, but it wasn't even close to the kind of money she made as a teen, gracing the covers of several magazines.

Unfortunately for Elena, and Sergio as well, her parents squandered the vast majority of her small fortune before she had even graduated high school. Because of this, Elena barely spoke with her parents. A phone conversation a couple of times a year, and dinner maybe once a year, was all the contact they had. No family Thanksgivings or Christmas Day celebrations for them.

Her parents had never apologized for what she considered embezzlement of her hard earned money. Instead, they said it was for the upkeep of the house and lifestyle that she had become so accustomed to.

Elena disagreed. Yes, it was used for the house and lifestyle. But not for her. It was for them. Sure, they doled out a generous allowance to her, much more than her friends ever got, but that didn't matter to her. It was her money after all. Her parents had quit working the moment her paychecks exceeded theirs, and they never looked back. In fact, they were still living off of what was left of the money, though to be fair, there wasn't much left.

And that was perfectly fine with Elena. During their last dinner together, about six months ago, her parents had asked them for money, citing the fact that they were just about out and had a mortgage to pay. Elena erupted in laughter, causing every set of eyes in the restaurant to be squarely focused on them. She didn't notice, and didn't care.

"You've got to be kidding me," she said once the laughter subsided. "You stole literal millions from me, gave me only a hundred dollars a week in compensation for my hard work, and now you have the audacity to ask me for money. Go to hell."

She stood up just as the appetizers were being placed on the table, and turned to the waiter. "You can cancel our orders," indicating her and Sergio with a nod of her head. "They are on their own regarding whatever they ordered. Come on, we are out of here."

Sergio took her hand and she led the way out of the restaurant, never looking back.

Elena hadn't spoken to her parents since. Not that they

haven't tried to contact her, but she blocked them on anything and everything she could think of.

Once, her cousin, Jennifer, called to plead her parents' case. Elena shut her down the second she realized what the call was about. That was the last time any family member tried to intervene in their relationship...or lack thereof.

CHAPTER 33

Sergio found Elena sitting in their breakfast nook, sipping on coffee. Her hair was not the usual perfectly coifed masterpiece he was used to. It looked like it hadn't been brushed since the day before.

She always wore a lime green long t-shirt to bed. This morning, she was still in it, wrapped in her yellow robe. The bright, cheerful colors did not match the mood on her face. And it wasn't like her to not be up and dressed for the day long before he was up in the morning.

She was an early bird, and always had been. Even as a teen, it wasn't unheard of for her to be up by 5 a.m., dressed in her favorite t-shirt and shorts, heading out for a long run. It helped keep her in shape, as well as run off all the teenage energy that she possessed.

Even in her mid-thirties, Elena went running a couple of days a week. It was one of her favorite things to do. Not that she needed it. The woman hadn't been an ounce overweight her entire life.

The front door snapped her out of her daydream.

Elena almost dropped the cup she had been holding when

she saw Sergio walk in. "Where the hell have you been all night? I've been worried sick." She stayed seated. She had been up most of the night and didn't have the energy required for standing.

"What time did you wake up?" Sergio wasn't fooling anyone. He was fishing and she knew it.

"Serg, just tell me where you were. Is there another woman?"

His eyebrows raised to an almost impossible angle. "What? No. I would never do that." This was at least the truth. He had never, and would never, cheat on his wife.

"Then what? Where were you and what were you doing?"

"I...I...went to..." Oh boy, this was going to be harder than he thought. He hadn't come prepared for an interrogation.

She did the 'hurry up' maneuver with her right hand, rotating it in a circle. "Went to do what?"

An acrid scent wafted her way. She drew it in through her nose, and crinkled it. "Why do you smell like smoke?" Taking in his appearance, now that her initial anger had subsided a bit, she looked at him from head to toe. "And why are you so filthy? Serg, what is going on here?"

He instinctively looked down at the clothes he wore. "We need to talk."

"Yeah, I would say so," she responded. Elena raised a bare leg and scooted out the chair next to her. "Sit."

Sergio dutifully did as he was told.

"I went to get our money."

Elena tilted her head and looked into his eyes. "What money, Serg?"

"Our money. You know, the rest of the duffle bag money that should have been ours in the first place." He couldn't meet her eyes.

"You mean the money that Tommy and Rosie have?"

"Had," he corrected. "I have it now."

"What do you mean? Why would they give it to you?" she asked.

"Because I asked them nicely."

"That doesn't make any sense," Elena told him. "What do you mean? I still don't know why they would give you their share of the money."

"It doesn't matter now anyway. I have the money and that's all you need to know. I hid it for now. You know, just in case someone comes looking for it."

"Where? Is it here at the house?"

"No, it's buried near our special spot. The tree we love so much. Well, actually by the boulder behind it. I didn't want it to be too obvious to anyone else that might hang out by the tree, you know?"

Something wasn't right. Elena could just feel it deep in her soul. Something sinister hung in the air between them, and she needed to find out exactly what that thing was.

"Okay...but you didn't answer my question. Why would Tommy and Rosie just give you their share of the money. We split it, fair and square."

Sergio slammed his palm on the table, causing Elena to jump. "No, not fair and square! That was our money all along. It never belonged to them, and they had no right to it!"

He stood and began pacing around the kitchen, circling the island that sat smack in the center of the room.

"Yes they did have a right to it." She thought for a moment. "At least as much right as we did anyway. We all stole that money. And we made a deal with them. So I don't understand any of this at all..."

Sergio stopped in his tracks just as he was passing the table that Elena remained seated at, and held his palm up, facing her. "Just stop. Stop asking so many questions. I told you what happened, and you need to just accept that."

Elena picked up the phone that was lying on the table in front of her. "I'm calling Rosie. At least she will tell me what really happened."

Sergio almost leapt over the table in an effort to get the phone from her, and grabbed it out of her hands.

A huff escaped Elena's throat. "What the hell, Serg? If you aren't going to tell me, then I know Rosie will." She reached her right hand out. "Now give me my phone back."

"No."

"No?" she asked, wide eyed.

"I need to tell you something else." Sergio sat back down in the chair next to her. "Tommy and Rosie are dead."

CHAPTER 34

Elena's jaw dropped. "What? No, that can't be true. You're lying. Why would you say that?"

Sergio averted his eyes and set the phone down on the table in front of him. No matter what he was capable of, no matter what he had done in the past, he had never felt much guilt, except when confessing something to his wife. She was his love. His rock. He would do anything for her.

And that's exactly what he had done. He had gotten the much needed money, so they could have a nice future together. Hell, Tommy and Rosie never needed it. They were doing okay, at least as far as he could tell.

Elena tapped his hand, bringing her husband back to the present. "Sergio, answer me. Why would you say that they are dead? It's not really true, is it? Please, tell me it's not true."

Elena took his chin in her hand and turned his face toward her. She looked into his eyes. "Tell me the truth. Right now."

"Yeah, yeah, okay. Yes, what I said is true. They are dead. Both of them."

"I don't believe you." Elena grabbed the phone from the

table and turned her body so that her back faced Sergio. She tapped the name Rosie Allen and put it on speaker, holding the phone in front of her. She squeezed the phone tighter as it rang, willing her friend to answer it. After four rings, it went to voicemail.

"This is Rose Allen. I'm out living my life. Leave a message and I'll get back to you at some point."

Elena tapped the red "End" button without leaving a voicemail. A single tear made its way down her cheek.

"It's not true. Tell me it's not true, Serg. Tell me!"

"I'm sorry."

Elena called again. And again. Each time was the same as the last. "Answer the damn phone!" she yelled. It made no difference.

Sergio sat in silence as his wife tried over and over to reach her best friend. He knew it was all in vain. Rosie was not going to answer. No matter how many times Elena called her, Rosie was never going to answer.

Elena dropped her phone on the table with a thud. She was focused squarely on her husband.

"You killed them, didn't you? You killed my best friend." Her voice was almost eerily calm.

He looked down at the table in front of him. "I'm sorry."

"She was my friend. How could you do that?"

"I'm s…"

Elena interrupted him. "Don't you dare say you're sorry again! Don't you dare."

Sergio looked at her red rimmed eyes as the love of his life cried her eyes out. He tried once to reach over and comfort her, and was rewarded with a slap to the face.

Sergio got up to fetch a box of tissues and placed it on the table in front of her. Elena shoved it out of the way and ran to their bedroom. Sergio knew better than to follow her.

Two hours later, Elena emerged. She found Sergio sitting

silently on the living room couch, just staring at the dark television. He knew that he had messed up, and was terrified that the love of his life might never forgive him.

She walked over and sat in the chair next to the couch. She looked at her husband. "You took a shower?"

He nodded.

"You never did tell me why you came home dirty and smelling of smoke. Did that have to do with the murders of my friends?"

Sergio flinched at her words, and nodded again.

"I don't want to know any more." She turned and walked out of the room.

CHAPTER 35

The county sheriff, James Carter, was a large man, by anyone's standards. At forty years old, he stood at exactly six feet and eight inches tall. His muscular build and height made him an imposing figure. He had dark skin and closely cropped hair.

The townspeople of Silver Lake had learned not to judge a sheriff by his cover.

Most people were intimidated by the sheriff because he was a no-nonsense sort of person. However, he could be extremely caring when the need arose and was one of the nicest people most had ever met. They only ever called him *Jimmy*. Nothing else, and that's the way he liked it.

The citizens of Silver Lake often gave a little tap on their horn and a wave when they passed him on his bicycle. He rode it the eight miles to work most days.

The sheriff could smell the distinct odor of a left over fire before he could see the cabin. It reminded him of camping with his parents at around ten or eleven years old. He smiled despite what he was about to walk into.

Climbing out of his 4x4, Sheriff Carter stood and stared

at the cabin. Or what was left of it. A few charred boards of what was once the frame, still stood. As did the fireplace and chimney, though they were just as soot covered as everything else.

A deputy and a few people from the fire department were milling around.

As he walked into what was left of the cabin, the sheriff spotted a blackened picture frame, lying on its face, at the foot of the fireplace. He surmised it was once on the mantel, as he picked it up and brushed away the soot with the sleeve of his jacket. Faces emerged in front of him. A man and woman, maybe in their early twenties. He wore a tuxedo and she was in a white wedding dress. They were standing on a beach, and they looked happy. He didn't recognize either face, but figured they were the owners of the pile of ashes now before him.

The sheriff handed the photo frame to a passing deputy. "Here, bag this."

"Yes sir."

"What do we have here?" The sheriff asked, joining the deputy, who was standing over two bodies.

Deputy Felix Jones flipped open his notebook. "Well the neighbor lady said these two are the owners of this cabin. Tommy...um Thomas, and Rose Allen."

"I see. And what else did she say? Is she the one who found them like this?"

"Yes," Jones replied.

The sheriff's eyes scanned the cabin and out the front of it. Most of the wall was in a charred heap at their feet. "We are out in the middle of nowhere. Were they expecting her over? I can't imagine she was just wandering by."

"She said she was walking her dog through the woods. Says she does that a lot. She sometimes stops and chats with the wife here. She said that as she got closer and closer, she came across all of this." The deputy made a sweeping gesture with his right arm.

"And?"

"She was shocked to find the cabin had burned down. Said she couldn't see it from her house. Anyway, she looked inside, because their car is in the driveway. That's when she saw them lying here."

"How come the fire department didn't report this?" Sheriff Carter asked.

Deputy Jones shrugged. "They didn't know about it, from what I understand."

The sheriff scanned the area. "How is that possible? I can still smell the gasoline. And this place is almost completely gone. That had to have been one helluva fire."

Deputy Jones pointed. "The fire department is here now, investigating."

"Okay, good. Go get more details about this when we are done here," Sheriff Carter ordered.

Deputy Jones followed on the sheriff's heels as he perused what was left of the cabin. He found the kitchen and looked around. Something caught the sheriff's eye. It was sticking out from underneath something charred beyond recognition. Fishing a pair of gloves from his pocket, he pulled them on, bending over to pick up the item.

"What do you have there?" the deputy asked.

Sheriff Carter turned it over in his hands. "I'm not sure. Looks like maybe a brochure or picture of some sort. There's not much left. It's probably nothing, but here, bag this, and the lab can see if they can figure it out."

Deputy Jones always carried evidence bags while at crime scenes. Even the most insignificant item could be meaningful. He took the paper and put it in a bag, handing it over to the young technician as she walked by.

"Is that it? The neighbor, I mean," the sheriff asked.

"Oh, she also said...that woman is quite a talker," he added, "she said that Rosie talked about their friends a lot. She has never met them, but I guess they are all 'attached at the hip,' or so she says."

"And do these friends of theirs have names?" The sheriff was getting a little annoyed at having to keep asking questions. He preferred when all of the information was provided without him having to keep prodding the conversation along.

"She said that the wife's name is Elena. She's kind of famous, I guess. And she thinks the husband is Sebastian or Samuel, something like that. It starts with an 'S' and that's all she remembers for sure. She said Rosie talked about Elena a lot more than about Elena's husband. She doesn't know their last names," Deputy Jones informed him.

"Then get on it. I want to know everything about the friends by the end of the day. Got it?" The sheriff raised his eyebrows.

"Yeah, got it." Deputy Jones turned on his heels and headed for the door area.

"Wait. What about family?" the sheriff added. "Do these two," he indicated the bodies on the remnants of the living room floor, "have parents, siblings, whatever?"

"I don't know. I asked the neighbor lady that, but she said that Rosie never mentioned anyone, other than both of their parents were dead. So, I don't know if there is any other family."

"Okay, find that out too," the sheriff ordered.

"Yep."

CHAPTER 36

"Before we go in, we need a story," Sergio told his wife. "We can't go in without figuring out what to say."

"Why do you think the sheriff wants to talk to us anyway?" Elena asked him.

"Tommy and Rosie. And the fire. What else?"

"Fire? There was a fire?" Elena looked toward the heavens. "Please god, tell me you didn't set my best friend on fire."

Elena locked eyes with Sergio. He turned away.

"Serg, you set them on fire?" Her eyes widen, pupils dilated, as if trying to take in something too terrible to comprehend.

"They didn't burn to death," he told her. "They were already dead by then. I just set the fire to cover up the evidence."

"Oh, that makes me feel so much better."

The sarcasm in her voice didn't escape him.

"So how did you kill them?"

"Do you really want to know?" he asked her, knowing that she didn't.

"No, not really. But we are going to see the sheriff shortly.

I'm sure I'm about to find out when we get there anyway. So you might as well tell me, so I can be prepared."

Elena crossed her arms in front of her, and gave Sergio that look. The one look of hers that he dreaded. It told him that she was determined. He knew that there was no way he was getting out of whatever it was that caused her to give him that look.

He shook his head. He figured he might as well relent. She was going to find out sooner or later. It could come from him, in the most gentle way possible, or it could come from the sheriff. He didn't know the sheriff, but figured that he was going to be much more direct.

Elena didn't deserve that. Her best friend was dead, and Sergio was to blame. He needed to do whatever he could to make the news easier to digest. If that was even possible.

"Serg, I'm waiting." Her foot tapped rapidly.

"Yeah, yeah, okay. I shot them. There, are you happy?"

Elena dropped her arms to her side. "Are you kidding me? You just asked if I'm happy that you shot my friends? What kind of monster are you?"

"I'm sorry. Truly I am. It was the only solution I could come up with to solve our problems."

"Sergio, when are you going to get it through your thick head that I don't care about the money. I would rather live destitute then be part of what you did to Rosie and Tommy. You're a horrible, horrible person, and I don't know if I can ever forgive you for that."

Sergio reached for his wife. She backed out of reach. "Don't touch me."

He pulled his hand back. "Okay. But we still need to talk. We still haven't figured out what we are going to say to the sheriff."

"Well, obviously, we can't tell him the truth," Rosie told him. "As angry as I am at you right now, you going to prison isn't going to help anything. Besides, if the whole truth comes out, we may be getting adjoining cells. So no, we can't tell them the truth."

"So, let's just play stupid," Sergio offered.

She tilted her head at him. "What do you mean?"

"I just mean, act like we don't know anything about it at all. We didn't know that they are dead. We didn't know that the cabin burned down. We don't know anything. You can pretend to be surprised when you hear the news, right? Throw in a few tears?"

"I don't like this. I don't like any of it," she told him, shaking her head at the thought.

"I know, honey, but we don't have any choice. It's either that or prison."

"I know that. Okay, fine, I can pretend not to know anything."

Sergio smiled.

Elena frowned.

"Don't smile at me. I'm still very very angry at you and will probably never forgive you. But I don't want you going to prison. I know you aren't a bad person. So I'll do my part to keep both of us out of trouble."

～

"Hi, we have an appointment with Sheriff Carter."

The woman behind the counter was a good seventy-five years old and one hundred pounds overweight. Her short gray hair was wiry and couldn't be tamed, no matter how hard she tried. Her name tag read *Doris*.

She dipped her head down and raised her eyes over the top of her reading glasses. "Your names?" She spoke with no emotion.

"Sergio and Elena Rivera."

"Sit down. I'll let him know you are here."

Doris proceeded to pick up the phone, spoke quietly for a few seconds, and placed it back in the receiver. "He'll be with you shortly."

Without waiting for a reply, she went back to whatever it was she was doing with a stack of folders in front of her.

The Silver Lake Sheriff's Department was very brown, Elena thought as she scanned the room. The walls were straight out of the 1970s, wood paneling and all. The floor had some attempt at a tiled pattern, also in shades of tan and brown. Even the ceiling, that was once maybe white, seemed to have settled into some weird brownish beige color. She wondered if it was from years of workers, sitting around smoking. No one did that anymore, of course, but once upon a time you couldn't walk into a building without being met with a wall of smoke.

It was another ten minutes before the phone buzzed in front of Doris. She picked it up, spoke softly once again, and finally looked their way. "The sheriff will see you now."

Sergio and Elena stood and watched as Doris heaved her large frame out of her chair, which squealed in protest. Or relief. They weren't really sure. She grunted and groaned as she waddled her way to the door and opened it for them.

They followed her, at an excruciatingly slow pace to the back of the station and toward the sheriff's office. She stopped about twenty feet before reaching his door, and pointed.

"He's in there." With that, she turned and started her slog back to the front desk.

Sheriff Carter despised using the interrogation room. He found it cold and barren. He much preferred to use his own office to talk with people. He wanted them to feel comfortable. When people were comfortable, they talked.

The sheriff rose as they entered, offering his right hand.

"Hello, I'm Sheriff Carter. Everyone just calls me 'Jimmy.' I know it's informal, but they've been doing it so long, since I was a desk jockey back in the day, that everyone is just used to it. So it's fine if you call me that too. It would be weird if you didn't."

"Jimmy?" Sergio repeated. "Your name is Jimmy Carter?" His smirk said it all.

Jimmy waved his hand in the air. "Yeah yeah, I know. My grandmother was a fan. So here we are." He smiled back, arms wide. He was used to the comments. It was old news by now.

"So, Sheriff, why exactly are we here?" Elena finally chimed in.

Jimmy looked over at Elena. He couldn't help but notice that she was striking. Looking over at her husband, he wondered what in the world she saw in him. Sergio was a decent looking guy, but nowhere near the league that Elena Rivera was in. She could clearly have her choice in men.

"Sheriff?" Sergio interrupted his thoughts.

"Oh sorry." He looked down at his notes. "I understand you two are friends with Thomas and Rose Allen?"

"Yes, why?"

"They are dead."

CHAPTER 37

"What?" Elena cried out. "That can't be true. Are you sure you have the right people?" She reached out and took her husband's hand. "Serg, tell me this isn't true."

Sergio looked at the sheriff, who just nodded his head.

"What happened?"

"Someone shot them. We found them this morning in their cabin. Have you been there? Have you been to the cabin?"

"Yes," Elena answered. "Do you know who did it?"

Sheriff Jimmy Carter leaned back in his oversized chair and contemplated the pair sitting before him. "Not yet. But we'll get to the bottom of it."

"Well, anything we can do to help." Elena leaned forward and pulled a tissue from the box on the sheriff's desk, wiping her eyes.

"We think it might be related to a home invasion at the cabin six months ago. Tell me what you know about that."

Sergio and Elena locked eyes for a moment, averting them quickly. "What home invasion?" Sergio asked.

The sheriff didn't miss much. And this time was no

different. He had learned early on in his career to observe people. You can find out so much more watching them, as opposed to listening to their bullshit stories. So he became a keen observer of his fellow human being.

Without missing a beat, the sheriff answered. "I heard you two were besties with the Allens. Are you sitting here telling me that you know nothing of a home invasion at their cabin?"

The door to his office opened and a young man stuck his head in. "Jimmy, sorry to interrupt, but we have a bit of a situation out here. We can use your help."

The sheriff stood, releasing an audible huff. "Sorry about this. I'll be right back, folks."

The moment the door closed behind him, Elena turned to her husband. "What do we do now?"

He patted the air down in front of him, and lowered his voice. "We can talk about this later, okay?" Leaning in, he whispered into her ear. "There may be eyes and ears in here. Watch what you say."

Elena bit her upper lip and nodded her head. The two sat in silence for a couple of minutes.

Scanning the sheriff's personal office, without leaving her chair, Elena noticed several family photos on his desk and on the shelves behind where he sat. She studied them from her chair, not daring to get up and walk behind the sheriff's desk.

"That must be his daughter." Elena nodded her head toward a photo of the sheriff with a little girl of about four or five years old, smiling proudly from her perch on a bored looking pony. Some photos had his wife in them, the pony one didn't.

Elena looked at all of the photos. They seemed like a happy family to her. Despite the circumstances they had found themselves in, she couldn't help but smile.

"She looks kind of familiar," Elena told her husband.

"Who?" Sergio pointed at one of the photos. "His wife? How would you know her?"

"No, not the wife. The daughter. I've seen that face some-where before. I just can't place it."

Sergio shrugged. "I don't know anything about that."

"Why would you? What does that even mean?"

The door opened before Sergio had a chance to respond.

"Okay folks, sorry about that. Had to put out a fire." He winced at the unfortunate choice of words. "I swear they can't do anything around here on their own." He rolled his eyes slightly, giving the impression that he was kidding.

He looked back and forth into the faces of Sergio and Elena. "So, where were we?"

CHAPTER 38

"Tommy and Rosie, I still can't believe it." Elena's lip quivered as she spoke.

Sheriff Carter didn't quite know what to make of Elena Rivera. Were those crocodile tears he was witnessing? She was still a mystery to him. But if there were any shenanigans going on, he would get to the bottom of them.

That's the kind of man he was. He didn't let any case go, until it was solved. No matter what. In fact, he had a near perfect record for solving cases. All except the one that haunted his dreams.

"I was asking you about the home invasion at the Allen's cabin several months ago. What do you know about that? And don't lie to me."

"Sir, really," Elena spoke up first, "we don't know anything. This is the first we are hearing about it."

"Mmm hmm. When was the last time you were at the cabin? Didn't you hang out with your friends often? That's what I heard?"

"What do you mean, that's what you heard?" Sergio asked.

"Who have you been talking to? Who would know anything about that?"

The sheriff gave them a one shouldered shrug. "No one in particular. It's just the scuttlebutt around town. So stop skirting the question. When were you there last?"

"Month ago. I don't remember exactly when, but I know it has been months. Not since right after they moved in," Elena told him. "They have been to our house, and we have gone out to dinner with them a few times, but it has been months since we have been to their cabin."

She took in a deep breath when she was done speaking, as it had all spilled out of her mouth in one long monologue. And it was true. Every word. They had not been to the cabin since that night. That fateful night that changed everything.

Sheriff Carter ignored her outburst and kept on questioning them. "So, are you telling me that you were not there the night of the home invasion? Because I heard differently."

The fact was that Elena's therapist had spilled her guts. She knew better, and she knew she might very well lose her license over it, but she couldn't help herself. Elena had told her about being at the cabin that night, and then being tied up, and the attempted assault on her. So when the deputies had shown up at her place of business, the therapist decided to tell them everything.

Of course, Elena had never mentioned shooting and killing the two men. She conveniently left that part out, so the therapist knew nothing about it. Therefore, the deputies knew nothing about it.

"We have told you over and over that we weren't there, and we don't know anything about any home invasion," Sergio told him. "This is the first time we are hearing about it. Tommy and Rosie never once mentioned it to us. So no, we weren't there, and we don't know anything."

"I see."

"But I do have a question for you," Sergio continued. "Why do you think there was a home invasion? I mean, did Tommy and Rosie report one? And why would anyone do that? I don't think they had any expensive jewelry or anything there."

"That's three questions actually," the sheriff responded.

Sergio couldn't fathom that his friends would put in a report at the sheriff's station for any reason. They had walked away unharmed, and a million dollars richer. So what could possibly be their motivation for putting in a police report?

Sergio relented. "Okay, three questions then."

"Well, this is gonna be easy. I can answer your questions all at once. No, we got an anonymous tip."

He was talking about the therapist, of course. But he couldn't let them know that. He had promised her complete anonymity if she spilled her guts. And she was happy to do so.

"What happened on the side of your head there?" The sheriff pointed to the area just above Sergio's left ear.

Sergio left hand instinctively reached up to rub the spot. He cursed himself for not letting his hair grow out a bit. It would easily cover up the scar.

"Oh this? It's nothing. I just, just…took a tumble when I was out jogging one day."

Sheriff Carter took a long look at Sergio. He couldn't call the man a liar, but he certainly didn't look like a jogger. But hell…what did he know? Maybe he just goes occasionally. Jimmy himself was an avid weightlifter.

Elena's heart rate began to race, and her hands felt clammy. "I…I need to use the restroom." She looked at the sheriff with raised eyebrows. She didn't think she needed permission, but felt the need to ask anyway.

He pointed to his left. "It's down that hall."

Elena couldn't get out of his office fast enough. She felt as if she couldn't breathe. Standing just outside his door, she bent over and took deep breaths, in an effort to control her breathing. Elena could feel eyes on her, but she ignored them. She briefly wondered if people often left Sheriff Carter's office in a panicked state of mind.

After a minute or two, she stood back up and turned to find the bathroom. She gasped at the poster in front of her.

CHAPTER 39

Right in front of Elena was a missing child poster. It was the same face she had just seen on a pony in the Sheriff's office only minutes before.

"Oh my god." She walked up to read it more closely.

It all came back to her.

A few years ago, three years according to the poster, Zoe Carter disappeared. She was only five at the time. Elena remembered it being big news in the area. She couldn't remember all the details, other than it being all anyone talked about for months. Then the story just kind of died out on its own.

She couldn't remember if the little girl was ever found or not, dead or alive. Maybe they left the poster up, as a reminder, or some other reason, she had no idea. She didn't dare ask the sheriff.

Elena looked toward the sheriff's office. He had a glass wall that looked out into the large area, where his deputies, and others, worked. He was watching Elena with interest.

She averted her eyes and headed straight for the bathroom, without so much as a glance back in his direction.

Elena looked in the bathroom mirror. Her face was blotchy. Not from crying, but from stress probably. The sheriff's questioning was starting to get to her. How in the world he knew about the home invasion at the cabin all those months ago, was a mystery to her. Only four people knew about it. Her, Sergio, Tommy, and Rosie. And those two weren't talking. So how could he know?

Sergio would never say anything, that's for sure. He was usually pretty tight lipped about secrets. He didn't go around telling people personal things. In fact, he was the one who reminded her not to tell the therapist about killing those two men.

Wait…the therapist. Could it have been her? She wasn't allowed to tell anyone what they talked about in therapy, right? At least that's the way she understood it. It had to be her. Who else could it have been?

After stalling for ten minutes, Elena couldn't hold off any longer. She had to return to the sheriff's office to continue answering questions. She splashed some water on her face and dried herself off.

"Are you feeling better, Mrs. Rivera?" Sheriff Carter asked as she took her seat next to her husband.

"Yes, thank you."

"Have you ever been the victim of a sexual assault, Mrs. Rivera?"

"What? No."

Now she knew for a fact that it was the therapist. She is the only one who Elena had ever spoken to about the attack. There was no way in the world her husband or friends would ever have told anyone about what that man had attempted to do.

Sergio's face turned red and sweat dribbled down the side of his head. "Why would you ask her that? What does any of this have to do with our friends getting killed?"

"I'm just asking questions. This is how we investigate crimes. We just want to find their killers."

Sergio stood. "We are leaving." He turned to his wife. "Come on honey. Don't say another word."

CHAPTER 40

Sergio pulled out of the sheriff's parking lot. "I need a drink."

Ten minutes later, he and Elena were settled into a corner booth in the back of their favorite watering hole. The sign out front just said 'The Pub,' and that's what everyone called it. They had no idea if it had another, official name or not. It had always been called that.

After ordering their drinks, Sergio spoke first. "What the hell was that?" he asked his wife.

Elena ran her fingers through the ends of her long hair. "What do you mean?"

"You running out of the office like that. You were in the bathroom forever."

She shrugged. "Sorry."

"Well don't do that again. It was very awkward in there with the sheriff alone. He didn't want to ask me questions without you being there. So we made small talk. It was horrible. Fishing? I don't like fishing."

"Sorry."

"Stop saying that."

"Sor..." She stopped mid-word, averting her eyes.

"Here you go folks. Enjoy." The bartender set their drinks in front of them and scurried off, without another word.

"I can't believe that Tommy and Rosie are dead," Elena told him. "What are we going to do?"

Sergio took a sip of his beer. "Do about what?"

Elena looked around. There were a handful of patrons at the bar, but as long as they kept their voices a bit low, no one was within earshot.

"You know," she lowered her voice to barely above a whisper, "the home invasion."

"Nothing. We do absolutely nothing. We weren't there and don't know anything about it, right?"

"Yeah, I guess. What about the money?"

"I hid it well. The cops won't find it," Sergio told her.

"Should we go get it?"

Sergio thought for a moment. "Um...no. We need to lay low for the time being. They could be following us. Just chill for now. Okay?"

Elena stared down into her drink. "Yeah, I guess. I don't want that money anyway. My best friends were killed for it." She raised her eyes and stared at her husband. "I don't want any kind of target on us. Whether that's from the police or from others who want that money, it doesn't matter. Don't you agree?"

"No one but us is getting the money. No way."

"You don't know that, do you?" she asked him.

"No, I don't know for sure. I don't want to talk about it anymore." Sergio raised his right finger in the air when the bartender looked their way.

A minute later, two more drinks were deposited in front of them.

"Hey Serg, did you notice the poster in the sheriff's office?"

Sergio took a long pull on his beer. "No. What poster?"

"The poster with the sheriff's daughter on it."

"Why would there be a poster with the sheriff's daughter on it?"

"Because she went missing three years ago," Elena explained.

"Oh. What's that got to do with us?"

She locked eyes with her husband. "It's got nothing to do with us. Why are you so callous? You can't feel bad for the man for even a minute when you hear something like that?"

Sergio shrugged. "I don't know him or her. So why do I care?"

Elena shook her head. "I don't believe this. And here I am wanting to have a baby with you. I guess it's a good thing it hasn't worked so far. You are unfreakingbelievable."

Elena grabbed her drink, downed the remaining half, and walked out of the bar. She didn't even look back.

About an hour later, Sergio stormed into the house. He found his wife in the kitchen with an open bottle of chardonnay.

"Why did you just walk out on me?"

"Because I was done speaking with you, that's why." Her words were a bit slurry.

"Did you walk home?"

"Yeah, and you...took your time getting here," she told him.

"I had an errand to run. It's the middle of the day and you are getting drunk."

"Yeah so? Want some?" Elena picked up the bottle and waved it around in the air, clanking it loudly on the side of the kitchen island she was sitting at.

Sergio reached for the bottle and took it from her hand.

"Okay, okay, let me have this before you break it and make a gigantic mess that I'll probably have to clean up."

"Fine, take it. I've had e...e...enough." She burped the words out.

Sergio laughed. "Yes you have." He set the bottle down on the counter, and took her hand. "Come on, you need a nap."

Trailing after her husband, Elena cried out. "Rosie is dead, Serg, dead!"

He wrapped his arm around her waist as they continued down the hallway. "I know honey, I know."

CHAPTER 41

Elena opened one eye to the early morning sun piercing through their bedroom window. Everything hurt. She didn't know how it was possible, but every inch of her body hurt. Her hair hurt.

The sudden lurching of her stomach got her moving fast. She made it just in time to the bathroom. But barely.

Once that was over, she shuffled back into their room. "Serg, I..."

Her husband was not there. She mulled over in her head for a moment as to whether she should go looking for him, or just climb back in bed, cover up her head, and stay there for the rest of the day.

The bed won.

Just as she started her climb in, the bedroom door opened.

"There you are. How are you feeling this morning?"

Elena stood up and turned to look at her husband. "Ugh, how do you think I feel? Did someone torture me last night?" She was only half kidding.

Sergio laughed. "Yeah, that's what a couple of bottles of wine will do to ya."

"I'm never drinking again."

He smiled, knowing that was not even close to being true. Elena didn't have a problem with alcohol, but she did like to have drinks with friends on occasion.

Sergio walked over and took her hand. "Come on, let's get some food in you. It'll make you feel better."

"Ew, I can't eat food right now."

"Yeah, okay," he laughed as he led her out the bedroom door.

Half an hour later, Elena had consumed a full plate of scrambled eggs, bacon, and toast, as well as a cup of coffee and some orange juice. Unlike a lot of drinkers, Elena thrived on large breakfasts after a night of drinking. It was the only thing that settled her stomach.

Sergio knew this about her, and was more than happy to cook for her. Once done, he grabbed a slice of toast and sat at the kitchen island across from his wife.

He couldn't help but notice how exceptionally beautiful she looked that morning. Sure, her hair was a mess, and her mascara was a bit smeary under her eyes, but those things were endearing. In his eyes, it made her even more beautiful than when she went to a lot of work to paint up her face and make her hair perfect.

Sergio took a bite of toast and a sip of his coffee. "How are you feeling now hon?"

"So much better, thanks. That really hit the spot."

Sergio smiled. "My pleasure. After everything that happened yesterday..."

Elena interrupted him mid-sentence. "Oh my god. I almost forgot. Tommy and Rosie are...are...dead." It took all she could muster to get the words out. Her eyes began puddling.

Sergio jumped up and ran around the island to wrap his arms around his wife. She placed her head on his shoulder as she cried it all out.

A few minutes passed and she pulled out of his embrace, wiping her eyes with the back of her hand. "God, I'm such a blubberer."

"No, honey, it's totally fine. Of course you are going to be upset. You just lost your best friend."

"I'm such a mess. I'm going to go take a shower." Without another word, she headed for the bathroom.

She wasn't sure why she was even still speaking to Sergio. Or in the same house as him, for that matter. She didn't hate him, and she didn't know why. But she was angry. So powerfully angry. She only spoke to him when necessary, as she needed time to figure out where to go from here.

And…she was kind of afraid of him, if she was being honest with herself. He was a murderer. Of her friends. That was something she was sure she could never forgive. But for the time being, she needed to keep her anger in check. It crossed her mind that she could be next on his hit list if things went sideways with them.

She took the time she had in the shower to cry again. She cried for her friends, and for what was certainly her own marriage that would be coming to an end at some point. She could not see herself growing old with someone capable of doing what Sergio had done. Not under any circumstances.

Thirty minutes later, Elena emerged. She was freshly showered, hair dried, and just a hint of makeup graced her face. Sergio was in awe at how effortless her beauty was.

She placed her laptop on the kitchen island and began typing. "I need to find out what happened to the sheriff's daughter."

CHAPTER 42

It didn't take long for Elena to find what seemed like ten thousand articles about Sheriff Carter's daughter, Zoe.

Ten minutes in, she yelled, "Serg, come in here!"

Seconds later, he emerged. "What, what, what's wrong?" His voice was high and agitated. "Did something happen?"

Despite everything that was going on, Elena giggled at his reaction. "Everything's fine, honey. Just calm down. I just wanted to tell you what I found out about Zoe."

He tilted his head to the right. "Who?"

"Zoe. You know, Zoe Carter, the sheriff's daughter?"

He walked over and once again sat in the chair across the kitchen island from her. "Oh yeah. What did you find out?"

She glanced down at the computer. "It looks like when Zoe was five years old, she was in her backyard playing alone, and it was about three years ago. When her mother went to call her to come back in, someone attacked her mother." Elena caught a hitch in her throat. "She's dead, Serg. They killed her."

"The little girl? Why would someone do that?"

Elena glared at him. "No Serg, not the girl, the mother.

Pay attention here. Someone killed the mother and took the girl."

"Oh. That stinks."

"Yeah, it does. There was a ransom demand, cause I guess the Carter family is loaded. But according to this article, no one ever called back to arrange for the money drop off."

"And the girl? What happened to her?"

"That's where this story gets really weird. No one knows. Zoe was never returned, dead or alive. She's just out there somewhere."

"And how long ago was that?" he asked.

"About three years. Then just nothing. There have been no articles about them in the past three years. That's weird, don't you think?"

Sergio shrugged. "I don't know. I guess if there are no new leads, then it makes sense that no one has written a follow up story about it."

"I should tell the sheriff how badly we feel about this," Elena said. "I just can't even imagine the hell he's going through."

"Elena, just leave it alone. It's not our problem."

"But what if that was our child? It would be hell. I think it might be comforting for someone to tell me they are still thinking about our child after so much time has gone by."

Sergio's lips pressed together in a tight line, and when he did open them, he spoke slowly. "I said to leave it alone."

At that point, he got up and walked out of the room without looking back. Elena's gaze followed him until he was out of sight.

CHAPTER 43

Two days later, Elena was right in the middle of making lasagne for dinner, when the front doorbell rang. Her hands, covered in marinara sauce were dangling in the air with the wide noodles ready to be layered in the baking dish.

Ugh, why do people insist on showing up right at dinner time?

"Serg! Can you get that! I'm covered in sauce," she called to other parts of the house. She hadn't laid eyes on him in a couple of hours, and had no idea where he had gone off to.

The doorbell rang again. "Serg!"

No response.

"Hang on!" she called toward the front door. She had no idea if they could hear her or not. Elena quickly rinsed her hands and grabbed the nearest kitchen towel, drying them on her way. She was still holding the towel when she pulled the door open.

Her eyes went wide.

"Hello Mrs. Rivera. Is your husband home?"

Standing before her was none other than Sheriff Carter and a younger man in uniform. It was the same deputy who had stuck his head in the sheriff's door the other day when they were there in his office.

"Uh, yeah, he's here somewhere. Come on in, I'll see if I can find him." She pointed. "The kitchen's that way, if you want to have a seat at the table. I'll be right back."

Elena found her husband lying on their bed, watching a baseball game. She closed their bedroom door behind her. "Serg," she whispered. Yep, there was some attitude in that whisper.

He picked up the remote and hit mute. "What?"

"The sheriff is here, and he doesn't look too happy. Get up. He wants to talk to us."

"What does he want?"

"How should I know? Just come on. Don't make me have to make small talk with them."

"Them?"

"There's a deputy with him too. Come on, get up," she ordered.

"Okay, okay, I'm coming."

Elena followed her husband down the hall. "I don't think I'm gonna like this," she said, her voice barely above a whisper.

"Hello Jimmy," Sergio greeted, sticking out his hand.

Elena gave him the side-eye. No matter how many people called him by his first name, she just couldn't bring herself to call the sheriff 'Jimmy.' That was just weird.

The sheriff took his hand with a firm shake. "Sergio. This is Deputy Felix Jones. You can call him Deputy."

Sergio smiled to himself. "Nice to meet you."

Once the pleasantries were done, all four sat down at the dining room table.

"So, Sheriff, what can we do for you today?" Sergio's voice was sickeningly sweet.

Elena made it a point not to react.

"Well, I'll get right to it. The autopsies are done and we are hot on the trail of the person who killed your friends."

The sheriff leaned back in his chair and crossed his arms. He looked satisfied, like he had just eaten the last bite of ice cream in the freezer, and there was nothing anyone could do about it.

Elena let out a breath of relief. "Oh thank goodness."

Sergio patted Elena's hand, in a comforting gesture.

"Who do you think did it?" Sergio asked, looking back and forth between the sheriff and his deputy.

"Well, here's the thing. We were able to match ballistics to one of the guns used in a series of robberies a while back. We are pretty sure who was using it, but we haven't been able to locate them just yet. We will though, you can count on that."

Sergio and Elena looked at each other, both trying their best not to show any emotion at all.

The sheriff was watching them. He was a keen observer of human behavior, and he was positive that these two had something to hide. Just what they had to hide was something he wasn't one hundred percent sure of just yet. But he was determined to find out.

Elena looked at the sheriff and noticed him watching her intently. She averted her eyes. *Damn, that didn't seem suspicious or anything*, she thought. *He's going to figure it out. We are damned for sure.*

Elena jumped up, needing a distraction. "Um, sheriff, would you like something to drink? We have coffee, soda, water? Deputy, how about you?"

"Yeah, sure," Felix Jones replied. "I'll take a diet soda, if you have it?"

"Coming right up. Sheriff?"

He waved his hand in the air. "Nothing for me, thanks."

A minute later, she returned with three bottles of water

and a diet soda. She set the drinks in front of everyone. "Sheriff, I brought you a water, just in case."

He gave her a slight smile. "Thanks."

"Of course."

Sheriff Carter continued. "I want to ask you again if you two know anything about the deaths of Thomas and Rose Allen? Anything at all?"

They both shook their heads. "No sir, we didn't even know they were dead until you called us in the other day," Sergio told him.

Sheriff Carter picked up the water bottle and took a swig. "Where were you two on the day they died?"

"Nowhere," Sergio responded.

The sheriff detected just a bit of snark in his voice.

"Nowhere?" the sheriff repeated. "You had to have been somewhere."

"Well yeah. I mean, we were here at the house, not out running around. So, we were…nowhere."

"Is there anyone who can corroborate your alibi?"

"Why do we need an alibi?" Elena asked. "Are we suspects? We didn't have anything to do with killing them, you know. They were our friends."

The sheriff looked into her deep brown eyes. "Everyone is a suspect, until they aren't. So, I'll ask again, is there anyone you saw that day that can verify you were here all day?"

"No," Elena responded. "I don't think anyone came over at all. It was just the two of us, doing some work around the house."

He looked at the couple for a moment. "I see."

CHAPTER 44

Doris poked her head in the sheriff's office door. He had been deep in thought, completing some reports that needed to get done. He hated paperwork. It was the worst part of his job. He wanted to be out in the field, talking to the citizens of his county, and arresting the bad guys. Sitting behind a desk, completing paperwork was not his idea of a good time.

But he knew it was a necessary evil. Without the detailed reports, they couldn't investigate properly, and they couldn't get convictions. So, he knew that he had to put everything down in excruciating detail.

He lifted his head when he heard the door open.

"Jimmy, some bodies have been found out in the forest," Doris told him. "Jones and a couple others are already on their way over. I called them right before I came in here."

The sheriff nodded. "Thanks, love."

She turned and headed back to her perch at the front desk, without another word.

Sheriff Carter didn't know what he would do without Doris. Sure, she could be cranky, and she was often very slow in getting things done. But she had been with the sheriff's department longer than he had. She knew her stuff. And when something needed to be done, she got that sense of urgency and made things happen. She often anticipated what he was going to do before he even did.

He was almost finished with his paperwork. Those bodies are already dead, he thought. No need to be in a big rush. Twenty minutes later, he slammed the folder closed, finally having finished with his report, grabbed his jacket and the folder, and headed out.

The sheriff dropped the folder on Doris' desk as he passed her by. "File this for me, please," he asked her.

"Of course." She reached up, holding a slip of paper. "Here's where they are."

He took the slip of paper, and tipped his head. "Thanks. Be back in a while."

The GPS coordinates that Doris gave him were perfect, as usual, and Sheriff Carter found the spot easily. He did have to park and walk in a little ways, before he found the spot. He heard the voices of his team before he saw them.

Deputy Jones spotted the sheriff walking up, and headed over to greet him. "Over here, Jimmy."

The two walked another few yards.

"So, who do we have here?" Sheriff Carter and Deputy Felix Jones stared down into the makeshift grave, deep in the woods.

"This would be Angelo Perez and Dante Davis." Jones told him. "Jennifer found IDs on them."

"The two we've been looking for? Well, well, isn't this interesting? Any weapons found with them?" the sheriff asked.

"Jennifer here found one gun and a knife."

She looked up and smiled from where she stood in the hole next to the bodies. "I'm still looking, but that's it so far."

"The weapons are with the investigators now." Jones

added. "I'm pretty sure the gun will match to the bullets found in that couple burned in the cabin the other day. The Allens."

"Why do you think that?"

"It's the same caliber," Jones replied. "And that cabin is so close. Since we don't get a lot of crime around here, I find it highly unlikely that the four murders are unrelated. Don't you think?" He raised his eyebrows in anticipation of the sheriff agreeing with him. He seemed to always be seeking some sort of validation from him.

A chilling breeze swept through the crime scene and Sheriff Carter pulled his jacket in tighter and rubbed his hands together. He suddenly wished that he had thought to bring gloves with him.

"Why is it so damn cold today?" The clouds swept over the tops of the trees, giving the entire area a dark foreboding feeling. It made him shiver.

Not expecting an actual answer, he continued, looking around at the forest. "Now that you mention them, aren't we pretty close to the Allen's cabin?" He looked around, trying to get his bearings.

"Uh, yes sir. It's about a mile or so that way." Deputy Jones pointed off in the distance.

The sheriff's eyes followed the direction the deputy was pointing in. "Yeah, that's what I thought."

The sheriff and deputy stood in silence, watching the investigation team work for a few minutes. They were combing the woods looking for any clue, not having much luck.

"Who found them?" the sheriff asked.

Felix Jones looked down at his notepad. "Um, some hikers. A man and woman. Their dog started scratching at the spot and, well, you can guess what happened next."

Sheriff Carter nodded his head.

"You need me to get them in the office for a talk with you?"

The sheriff shook his head. "I don't think that'll be necessary. It's doubtful they known anything further. But keep their info, just in case."

The coroner reached her hand out to get the sheriff's attention. "Jimmy, a little help here?"

"Of course." He reached down and easily lifted her one hundred and ten pound frame out of the hole in the ground.

She brushed the dirt from her pants and then wiped her hands together, looking around at the forest surrounding them. "Why is it so dang cold today? I'm going to freeze my ass off out here. Why does this sort of thing never happen when it's seventy-five degrees out?"

The sheriff smiled to himself. He always appreciated Jennifer's snappy personality. Truth be told, he had a bit of a crush on her. But she didn't seem to notice at all, so he kept that little bit of news to himself.

"All right," the sheriff responded. "That's a start."

"Jimmy, there's something else you need to know," she continued. "That is not a fresh grave." She pointed and all eyes travelled to the hole in the ground. "Those bodies are several months decomposed. And they were both shot. I can tell you that right now. I'll know more once I get them on my table."

"Is that right?" The sheriff looked off in the direction of Tommy and Rosie's cabin. "This investigation suddenly got very interesting."

"I also think that the grave was dug up recently and reburied."

The sheriff raised his eyebrows. "What? How would you know that?"

"Well, I'm not entirely positive, but the dirt around it seems like it was recently disturbed, ya know? If they were buried here six months ago, and no one had bothered it, then the ground would be packed in pretty tightly, from rain, people and animals walking over it, and whatnot. But that wasn't the case. It was pretty soft, and just had the look of fresh dirt." She shivered in the chill. "Do with that information what you will. I just wanted to let you know."

"Thanks Jennifer, that's helpful. It gives us a jumping off point."

She nodded and smiled. "No problem, Jimmy. Happy to help."

"Also," she continued speaking, "I didn't find any other weapons, just the gun and knife that you already know about. So I'm pretty sure that's it," she told the two men standing with her. "And to what the deputy here said about the gun being used on those two people who burned up in the cabin fire? Yeah, no. It wasn't this gun. This one has been buried here for months. You'd have to do some more testing, as I'm not a weapons expert, but that gun doesn't look like it has been disturbed for a long time." She threw up her arms. "But that's just my opinion. You guys do what you need to do to verify that."

The sheriff turned to his deputy with raised eyebrows. Deputy Jones shrugged.

Jennifer continued speaking, ignoring the exchange she just witnessed between the two men. "I just think it's odd that there was only one gun on them. Men like them don't usually carry out crimes with just a knife on their hip. Don't you think that's strange, Sheriff?"

He turned to his deputy. "Jones, get the Riveras into my office by the end of the day. I need to talk to them."

CHAPTER 45

Sergio Rivera led the way into the sheriff's department, Elena in tow. With his teeth clenched and his eyebrows narrowed, he walked right up to Doris at the front desk.

"Apparently we have been summoned by your boss to come into this hellhole once again. I want to get this over with, so tell him we are here. Now." He clicked his tongue for emphasis.

At seventy-seven years old, and having worked at the sheriff's office her entire career, Doris had seen it all. From entitled teenagers, who didn't understand that they could get into trouble for their actions, to old men, who were so intoxicated that they couldn't stand on their own. Usually that resulted in having to call the janitor in. She preferred the teenagers.

One man, in his mid-fifties or so, was so high on something that he lunged himself across her desk and wrapped his hands around her throat before anyone could stop him. She was gasping for air for a good twenty seconds before they were able to get something in front of his throat and force him off of her.

She had bruises on her neck for two weeks, and she swore at that moment that she was going to retire before the end of the year.

Well, that was ten years ago, and she just couldn't figure out how she would make ends meet if she retired. She chastised herself often for not having the forethought to save money for her old age. Their department was so small, that they didn't offer pensions to their employees. And the pittance she got from Social Security was definitely not enough to live on.

After a lot of soul searching, she figured that she would just have to work until the day she died. She really couldn't see how it would end any other way.

So, when Sergio came at her desk, guns blazing, she didn't even look up at him, until she was done completing the form in front of her. She squinted at the form, taking her time. It gave her day just a little bit of pleasure to stall the jackass in front of her.

Eventually she realized that she didn't have her dark rimmed reading glasses on that hung from a silver chain around her neck. She lifted them, still ignoring the man before her.

He leaned in. "Um, excuse me. Did you hear me? We need to see the sheriff. Right now."

She looked up at him over her glasses. "Mr?..."

He rolled his eyes. "Rivera. Sergio Rivera."

"Yes, Mr. Rivera. I remember you now. Have a seat over there, and I'll let the sheriff know you are here." She pointed squarely at the benches on the far wall.

"We are not having a seat over there." He indicated the benches with his right thumb over his shoulder. "We don't have time for this. If the sheriff wants to talk to us, he needs to get out here right now, or we are leaving. Got it?"

"Serg, let's just go sit down and wait. It's fine." Elena took his arm and tried to guide him to the benches.

He jerked his arm from her grasp.

For a woman of her age and girth, Doris hefted herself out of her chair in a surprisingly swift motion. "Now, Mr. Rivera, I…"

"It's all right, Doris, I got this."

All three looked over to see the sheriff standing off to the side, leaning against the door frame, with his arms crossed in front of him. A smirk graced his face. His body seemed to fill the entire doorway. He was an imposing man for sure.

The sheriff stood up straight and dropped his arms to his side. "Now, Mr. Rivera, are you finished berating this lovely lady, or do you have more to say? Because I'd like to hear if you have anything else you would like to say to her."

Sergio stood silently.

"No? Cause I'm all ears." The sheriff knew he was taunting Sergio, and he didn't care.

Sergio glanced at Doris and lowered his eyes for just a moment, looking back up at the sheriff. "No, I'm done. Why are we here?"

"We'll get to that. But before we do, you need to apologize to Doris, don't you think? She was just doing her job, and she has been doing it for a long time. She has forgotten more than you will ever know. And, every single day she has to put up with jackasses like you, and no one should have to do that. So, apologize." The sheriff crossed his arms in front of his chest again.

Elena was standing a bit behind her husband at that point. She smiled to herself.

Sergio could see that nothing was going to get done unless he did as he was told. He let out a huff. "Okay, fine. Doris, I'm sorry for yelling. It was uncalled for."

Doris only nodded in response.

The sheriff stood to the side. "Not really a heartfelt apology, but I guess it'll have to do. Okay, now that that's done, let's go have a chat, shall we?"

Doris and Elena traded smiles and Elena followed the men.

CHAPTER 46

Sergio and Elena follow the sheriff dutifully past the front desk, and the disapproving eyes of Doris, into the open area where all of the officers sat. All eyes were on them. Elena could feel the heat in her cheeks.

She was used to men looking at her, but this was something else entirely. Their gazes showed what? Anger? Hatred? Suspicion? She wasn't sure, but she didn't like it. Elena focused her eyes squarely into Sergio's back and did her best to pay no attention to those around her.

As they walked, Sergio leaned back to whisper into his wife's ear. "Just be quiet please. I know what to say. Let me handle this."

Elena pulled back from him and looked her husband in the eyes. She did not appreciate his demeanor at all, and the fact that he was telling her to keep her mouth shut. It wasn't the 1950s after all, and she was perfectly capable of handling herself in pretty much any situation. She had seen, and gone through, quite a bit during her time as a model. The people she came into contact didn't always have her best interests in mind.

Besides, they had nothing to hide. *Well, mostly nothing,* she thought to herself.

Instead of taking the pair to his office, this time he led them to the interrogation room. It was a small department, and they only had one room for questioning suspects. It also had glass walls, so that anyone in the department could keep an eye on what was happening in that room.

"Sorry for this folks," the sheriff began, "normally, I like to talk to people in the comfort of my office. But there's a lot more room in here for this sort of thing."

"What sort of thing?" Sergio asked him. He stood his ground, not wanting to give the sheriff anything to be suspicious about.

The sheriff pointed to the table. "This. Mugshots. Lots of them. I need you to go through all these books."

He looked up into the sheriff's eyes. "What for?" Sergio asked.

"To see if anyone here looks familiar."

"I don't understand," Elena chimed in. "Look familiar in what regard? What is going on here?"

"He thinks we are lying to him," Sergio told her. "He thinks we were involved with Tommy and Rosie's murders, and that we'll just pick some random people to blame." He looked the sheriff in the eyes. "Isn't that right, Jimmy?"

The sheriff flinched. He was used to everyone calling him 'Jimmy.' But somehow, some way, the way Sergio said it, made his skin crawl. Suddenly, he didn't like suspects using his name so much.

The sheriff put it out of his mind, and shrugged. "I just want you to look at these photos and tell me if you see anyone familiar. Nothing more, nothing less. There's no hidden agenda here."

"No," Sergio told him. "We are not wasting the next

several hours on this stupid shit. Why don't you just get to the point?"

The sheriff stuck his head out the door of the interrogation room. "Jones, bring in those photos from my desk."

The three occupants stood in silence until the deputy returned.

The sheriff took the photos from the deputy and laid five mugshots on the table in front of them. "How about these? Anyone you recognize?"

Sergio and Elena leaned over and perused the five photos. Elena took in a quick breath and looked at her husband. This did not go unnoticed by Sheriff Carter. *That woman would be a terrible poker player*, the sheriff thought. *Or witness, for that matter.*

He turned to Elena. "Do you have something you would like to say? You recognize one of these guys?"

She looked at her husband and he widened his eyes at her. Elena shook her head quickly. "No sir. I don't recognize anyone."

"Are these the people who killed our friends?" Sergio asked.

Ignoring the question, Sheriff Carter spoke up. "We found the bodies of two of these men in recently disturbed graves not far from the Allen's cabin. Those two there." He pointed at the photos of Angelo and Dante.

"Okaaay…so what does that have to do with us?" Sergio asked.

"They were our top suspects in the murders of your friends, but something interesting was discovered when we found the bodies."

"What?" Elena asked. Sergio gave her the side-eye and she slammed her mouth shut.

"Based on the decomposition, the medical examiner has told us that the suspects have been dead for several months."

The sheriff stood silently after that, watching the couple for their reaction.

Sergio didn't even flinch. "How can that be possible? Tommy and Elena were killed only a few days ago. That means these can't be the right killers. So why are you showing us their photos?"

Elena marveled at how well her husband handled himself under pressure. It was a little scary, if she was being honest with herself. Lying just seemed to come second nature to Sergio. It solidified the fact that she never wanted him to be an influence to any child she might have.

CHAPTER 47

"That's my question exactly," Sheriff Carter said in response to Sergio. "How can two men who died months ago be responsible for killing your friends a few days ago?" He tapped his right index finger on his temple. "It's a puzzler."

Sergio and Elena stood quietly, not really knowing the best way to respond to what the sheriff just said to them.

"Wanna know what I think?" Sheriff Carter asked.

They both nodded tentatively, not sure that they really did want to know what he thought.

"I believe that whoever killed your friends knew where these bodies were buried in order to get the gun. Strangely enough, there seems to be a missing gun from the gravesite. Odd, don't ya think?"

Ignoring her husband's earlier order to stay quiet, Elena decided she was done with that nonsense. *This is the twenty-first century for heaven's sake.*

"Sheriff, what exactly does any of this have to do with us, and why do we keep getting called in?"

"It means we are looking for somebody who killed four

people. Your friends the other day, and these two men six months ago."

"Oh." It was the only thing that she could say. Her husband didn't say a word. She had a feeling that they were going to have a discussion about this later. *Oh well, that's a problem for later.*

"And we think we found them," the sheriff added.

Both Sergio and Elena looked at him, then at each other, then back to him.

"You mean us?" Sergio asked, pointing at his own chest. "Do you think we did it? That's just asinine." He turned to his wife and took her hand. "Come on, we're leaving."

As the pair approached the door to exit the interrogation room, the sheriff stepped in front of them, blocking their exit.

"What are you doing? Unless we are under arrest, you need to get out of our way," Sergio demanded.

"We are just here talking," Sheriff Carter responded. "I would like to tell you exactly what I think happened."

"Why? We had nothing to do with it. So I don't know why you even want us here in the first place."

"Didn't you though?" The sheriff folded his arms in front of his chest as he spoke.

"No, we didn't!"

The sheriff uncrossed his arms and indicated the chairs at the table next to them. "Why don't we all have a seat, and I'll tell you a little story."

"I don't think that's a good idea. Please move so we can leave."

"I'd like to hear what he has to say," Elena chimed in. "They were our friends. Don't you want to know what happened to them?"

She ignored the death of the two men who had attacked

them all those months ago, and hoped that the sheriff would only concentrate on Tommy and Rosie.

Sergio's teeth clenched together as he did his best not to blow up at her. All he wanted to do was get out of there. And as fast as possible. But now what? His wife had pretty much just told the sheriff that they would stay and hear him out. He thought about it for a moment. With his shoulders slumping, he pulled out a chair and sat down. Elena and the sheriff followed suit.

"Okay, here we are, ready to listen. What is it that you so badly need to tell us?"

"I think your wife here killed two of these men."

"Wha...wha...what?" Elena responded. "I didn't... couldn't...I don't even know..." she stammered.

Sergio put his hand on his wife's knee and gave it a gentle squeeze. "It's okay sweetheart, let me deal with this."

Oh this should be good, the Sheriff thought.

Sergio shot to his feet and locked eyes with the sheriff. "Have you lost your damn mind? My wife could never hurt anyone. I can't even fathom why you would say that. Why? Why would you even think that? We don't know those men you found!"

Sheriff Carter smiled at Sergio's outburst. "Mr. Rivera, please sit down, so that we can discuss this like adults who are not throwing temper tantrums."

Sergio's neck heated up and traveled up into his face. He wiped off his forehead with the back of his hand, while he did as he was told and sat back down next to Elena. She looked over at him and bit her lower lip. He wasn't sure if she was upset by his outburst, or amused by it.

In as calm of a voice as he could muster, Sergio spoke up. "Why do you think my wife killed these men here?" He indicated the row of photos in front of them.

"Not all of them, just two. Just the ones we've been

talking about on your far right there." The sheriff pointed once again at their photos.

Both Sergio and Elena stared at the photos of the two men.

"We think your wife killed those two men, or at least one of them, six months ago during the home invasion at the cabin and the assault on her."

Elena slammed both of her hands on the table in front of them, causing one of the photos to fly up and land on the floor at the foot of their chairs. "There was no assault! I don't know how many times I need to say it. I just…"

"Honey!" Sergio interrupted, before she said something neither of them wanted her to say. "Just calm down. Let's take a deep breath."

She looked at her husband and nodded. "Yeah okay, fine." She took a couple of deep breaths as she attempted to calm down like he suggested. It wasn't working.

Elena Rivera was angry. More angry than she had probably been in her entire life. Not at Sergio. Though he was a high second on the list, and she'd get back to him shortly. At that very moment, she would wrap her hands around her therapist's throat, if she got the chance. How dare that woman break a confidence and tell the sheriff what she had shared in therapy.

Therapy was supposed to be a private space…a safe place, to talk about all of your fears and emotions. Elena had done exactly that. Now, because of that woman, she was being accused of murder.

When they were done with all of this, Elena was going to find a lawyer, and sue the stuffing out of that woman. When Elena was done with her, if she wasn't in prison for what she did, then the only job she would be able to get would be wearing a uniform and asking if they would like fries with their burger.

CHAPTER 48

The sheriff turned to Sergio. "And we think that you killed your friends the other day."

"That is insane," Elena told the sheriff. "What possible reason would my husband have to kill our friends?"

"Maybe to keep your secret?"

"What secret?" Elena asked. "Nothing happened! There is no secret to keep."

"We found what we believe is your wife's DNA on one of the suspects."

Aw crap. It hadn't crossed either of their minds that her DNA might be on that disgusting excuse for a human being. They had fought, and she had gotten scratched. So yes, now that she thought about it, her DNA probably was on him. *Oh god, I'm going to prison.*

Regardless, she had to try to get them looking in another direction.

"How is it possible for my DNA to be on someone when they didn't assault me?"

"Honey, let me handle this," Sergio repeated with wide

eyes aimed at his wife. He placed his hand gently on her back.

She was blowing it, Sergio thought. She was going to say something that put us in that cabin that night, and he needed to put a stop to it before that happened.

Sergio took a deep breath, wanting to calm down his rapidly beating heart. "So you don't even know for a fact that my wife's DNA is on those men. Do I have that right? You're just fishing here?"

The sheriff nodded. "Yeah, that's what we do." He saw no point in lying about it. "A big part of our job is to ask questions so we can figure out what happened. This can't be news to you."

The sheriff had skillfully turned it around on Sergio Rivera, and the man looked away.

Sheriff Carter ignored Sergio and turned to Elena. "Mrs. Rivera, if you would be willing to give us a DNA sample, we can put this mystery to bed. What do you say?"

"I, uh..." She looked at her husband with questioning eyes.

"Even if her DNA is on them, and I'm not saying it is, that doesn't prove anything."

"It proves that she had contact with them," the sheriff responded. "So that makes it a pretty good jumping off point for us, don't you think?"

Sergio and Elena locked eyes. Neither said a word.

The sheriff ignored what he had just witnessed.

"So, unless she was having an affair with the suspect, and we are guessing that isn't the case, then it proves you lied about everything. You said you weren't there, clearly you were. It gives you motive. At least, as far as these murders are concerned."

He paused to see what reaction he was getting. Both Sergio and Elena sat stone-faced.

"And since all of this happened at your friends' cabin, it's not unreasonable to assume that because your friends were witnesses, that they were killed the other day to ensure their silence."

"Their silence about what?" Sergio asked.

"About the sexual assault. Your wife is clearly very upset, even talking about it."

"That's absurd. You're fine, right honey?"

"Yeah," she responded, her voice barely above a whisper.

"Right now, your wife is the only one we can prove had contact with these two men. So she is the one we are focusing on as being involved in all four deaths."

"That's absurd," Sergio told them, point blank.

"Is it?" Sheriff Carter asked.

"Yes, of course it is. She's not a killer. She's the sweetest person I have ever known. It just isn't in her to do anything like that. And you think she killed four people? Have you lost your mind?"

"I didn't say that she killed four people. I said that I think she killed Angelo and Dante, and that *you* killed your two friends to cover all of it up." The sheriff looked over at Elena to gauge her reaction. "Am I not being clear here? I thought I was being very clear."

She shrugged.

"I have a court order compelling you to give us a DNA sample, Mrs. Rivera."

Elena started breathing deeply with her hand over her heart. It was racing, and she was doing her best to calm it down.

Sergio placed his hand gently onto Elena's back once more. "Honey, are you all right? You are white as a sheet."

"Can I...have...some water?" Her words were said between breaths.

"Yes, of course."

Sheriff Carter flagged down one of the department's employees and made a drinking gesture, without ever leaving his seat. A minute later, a cup of water appeared.

Elena drank it greedily. It helped some. Once she had calmed down, and her breathing returned to almost normal, the sheriff repeated himself. "Elena we need to get your DNA. It'll be painless, just a simple cheek swab. We'll get that taken care of now. Can I call in the tech to take care of it?"

"I killed those two men. But I don't know who killed Tommy and Rosie," Sergio blurted out.

CHAPTER 49

Sheriff Carter's eyes snapped to Sergio's. "What did you just say?"

"Those bastards attacked my wife and they had guns. So I killed them. I'm not sorry that I did it, and I would do it all over again. I'm prepared to give a formal confession right now."

Elena's jaw hung open. "I can't let you do this," she told her husband.

Sergio narrowed his eyes at her. "Not another word. Stop talking right now, and let me handle this."

She ignored him. "One of the men tried to rape me. That's why you will find my DNA on him. But I got a hold of his gun and shot him. It was self-defense."

Sergio's lips went pencil thin and he shook his head. "I told you to stop talking. Let me handle this."

Sergio was never one for letting others make their own decisions. This was especially true for his wife. The man liked to be in charge, and that's how it was in every aspect of his life.

Sure, he loved Elena, more than ever. But as far as he was

concerned, she was not the type to make good decisions. He needed to be there to help her out with that. He was still salty about her allowing her parents to pilfer her modeling money, and he never let her forget it.

The sheriff looked at Sergio. "Sir, let her speak. If you don't, then I will have you removed from this room." He raised his eyebrows. "Understand?"

"Sheriff, she is wrong. Don't listen to her," he tried to argue.

"Mr. Rivera, I'm warning you. I'm more than happy to interview your wife alone. So if you want to stay, you will need to shut the hell up. Do you understand or not?"

Sergio's eyes dropped to the table in front of him. "Yeah, I understand."

"Okay now, Mrs. Rivera, what about the other suspect? Did he also try to rape you?"

She couldn't look Sheriff Carter in the eyes. "No."

"You need to stop talking," Sergio blurted out.

"Mr. Rivera, you are getting on my last nerve."

Sergio held up his palms in the air, facing the sheriff. "Okay, okay, I'll be quiet. I promise."

"Serg, I can't do this anymore. We need to tell the truth. It's eating away at me." She looked up to the sheriff. "I killed him too. He deserved it."

"If he didn't assault you, then why did you kill him?"

"Because I was terrified. I thought he would also rape me. I felt threatened by him. He had a gun. He had tied up me and our friends. All of us. I was afraid."

"I see."

"But neither of us killed our friends," she added. "We don't know anything about that."

Sergio jumped in. "Please, don't listed to her. I'm the one who killed those two men for attacking my wife. Leave her out of this. It was clearly me defending her."

No matter how much Sergio liked to be in charge, and make decisions for her, and others, he couldn't let her go to prison for just trying to stay safe from two men who meant her harm.

The sheriff sat quietly, thinking. During that time, neither Sergio nor Elena said a word. They just looked at him, and each other, wondering which one, or if both of them, would be arrested that day.

Sheriff Carter stood. "I need to make some phone calls. You two go home. We have some more investigating to do. We will be watching though, so don't even think of going anywhere. I'm sure we'll have more questions for you. If this does turn out to be self-defense, that will be up to the D.A. to decide what to do about it."

Sergio and Elena couldn't get out of the sheriff's office fast enough.

Without making a conscious effort, Elena glanced over at the poster of missing Zoe Carter. No matter what they were going through, it broke her heart that the poor little girl never came home. She wondered how the sheriff had survived something so horrific.

Doris watched them with interest as they blew past her, barely glancing her way.

CHAPTER 50

The car ride home was tense. They could both feel it in the air. Neither spoke for several minutes.

"Are you not going to talk to me now?" Sergio asked his wife.

"They were our friends. I don't know if I can forgive you for any of this."

"Then why did you cover for me?" he asked. "You could have told them that I killed Tommy and Rosie, but you didn't. Why?"

Elena stared out the car window at the fast moving scenery. The day was gloomy. Clouds hovered dark and ominous above, threatening to spill a rainstorm on them at any moment.

"Hey, did you hear me?"

Without turning toward him, she replied. "Yeah, I heard you. I don't know why I covered for you. Maybe I shouldn't have. I'll probably go to hell for letting you get away with it."

Sergio's eyes rolled to the ceiling. "Don't be so dramatic. You aren't going anywhere. You did what you needed to do to keep our family safe."

Elena whipped her head toward the driver side of the car. "What family? You and I are not a family. Maybe we never were."

"Don't say that. I love you. We'll still have that baby some day. I know it. It's going to happen, trust me."

Elena focused back on the impending storm. The barely perceptible shake of her head at what her husband had just said, was not noticed by him. A baby. They were never going to have a baby, and she knew it. It just wasn't in the cards for them.

"What am I going to do without Rosie?" she asked aloud, not really expecting any answer from him.

Sergio slammed both hands on the steering wheel, causing Elena's head to snap around and stare at him. "They weren't our friends. They were greedy bastards. That wasn't supposed to ever be their money in the first place."

"Why not? We agreed to share it fifty-fifty. Why do you think they didn't deserve any of it? It was hidden in their walls after all!" Rosie yelled right back. "In fact, they are the ones that didn't have to share it with us!"

"When I hired Angelo and Dante, they were just supposed to go in, tie us all up to make it look good, get the money, kill Tommy and Rosie, and get out of there. But noooo...that jackass, Dante, decided on his own to assault you. I should never have hired him. I knew that he was a loose canon. He probably figured he'd just kill us too and take all the money."

Sergio tried to gauge Elena's reaction, but so far she sat stone faced, staring at him.

"When you killed Dante, and then Angelo, it ruined the entire plan. So part of this is your fault. He never raped you. You didn't have to kill either one of them."

Elena's mouth dropped open. "What?" she asked, horrified.

"We could have walked away with all of that money, except for the small fee I planned to give the guys," he added.

Her ears couldn't believe what she was hearing. Sergio had planned the home invasion and robbery himself?

"You did this?" Elena asked him, shocked at what she had just heard coming out of his mouth. "It was you who put us all in danger? He tried to rape me! Then you killed our friends. All of that was you? You bastard! I hate you and will never forgive you for this. Not ever!"

"All right, all right, just calm down." He patted the air with his right hand, while keeping his left on the steering wheel.

"I didn't go over there to kill Tommy and Rosie the other night, but they wouldn't give me more money. That was my money. It was never supposed to be theirs in the first place. I had no choice but to kill them. I did this for you. You can see that, right?"

Elena saw the look on his face. It was startling. She could see the desperation, and it frightened her. If the man she was supposed to love was capable of everything that he had done, then what was stopping him from killing her. She could very well be next on his list. Then he wouldn't have to share the money. It would be all his.

She needed to do something to protect herself. Sergio was deranged. She could see that now.

Elena yanked off her seatbelt as the car turned into their driveway. "Yeah, of course. You...you did what you...had to do." She would say anything to pacify him right then. She jumped out of the car and got to the house before Sergio had even climbed out.

"Honey, what's wrong?" he called, walking into the house a couple of minutes later and finding her sitting on the living room couch. "It was all just a huge mistake. It wasn't supposed to happen like it did. You can understand, can't you? And forgive me, right? Elena? Please baby, tell me that we can move on from this."

CHAPTER 51

Sergio sat on the couch next to his wife and put his arm around her shoulders. She scooted over and leaned forward, causing him to drop his arm and pull it back. "Are you mad at me?"

Elena turned to face him, locking eyes with him. "Are you seriously asking me that question? How can you be so thick? You are surprised that I'm upset and angry at you for what you did?"

"Look, I'm sorry. I know they were our friends, but…"

"No!" Elena interrupted him. "They were MY friends, not yours. If they were your friends, you would not have killed them over some money."

"That is not just *some* money. It's going to change our lives," he tried to explain.

"I don't care about the money! How many times do I need to tell you that? I want my friends back."

"Honey, I'm sorry. Really. I wish I could take it back, but I can't. Do you think you can ever forgive me?"

Elena sat in silence.

Sergio scanned the room, thinking for a moment. "You

know what, let's sell this house and move to Wyoming, like we talked about. I've always wanted a big ranch out in the middle of nowhere. No one will have any idea where to find us. We have a lot of money now and can do whatever we want. You like chickens, don't you? Fresh eggs every day?" He caressed her hand. "You'd like that, wouldn't you?"

Elena shrugged, playing along. "Yeah, I guess. How would that work? We have our house here and jobs."

"We sell the house and quit our jobs. We don't need the money. A million dollars will go a long way in Wyoming. We can always get part-time jobs if we need to. Come on, what do you think?" His eyes were wide and hopeful.

"Well..." Elena hesitated. "Moving to Wyoming does sound heavenly. I don't know if I can live here now anyway."

"I know, and now that we have money, we can go anywhere we want. So, you are saying yes?"

Elena nodded. "Yes. Let's get away from all of this and go to Wyoming."

Sergio jumped up off the couch and held out his hand. Elena took it. He pulled her up to face him and twirled her around right there in the living room. Elena squealed with delight.

"But what about the sheriff," she asked. "He isn't going to just let this go. One or both of us are probably going to prison."

"Not if we leave first," he told her. "We can hire an attorney to sell the house for us, maybe put it in a trust, or whatever. I don't really know how it all works. But I'm sure I can find someone who will do what we want without alerting anyone to where we are. I know people."

She stood still and looked at him. "You know people? Who did I marry? Do I know you at all?"

Sergio shrugged. "I'm still the wonderful person you

married. But yeah, there's always someone willing to help. For the right price that is."

"I see." She turned and headed toward the front door. "I'm going to go get us some dinner to celebrate. When I get back we can make plans okay? What do you want?"

"Surprise me."

Elena grabbed her car keys and closed the front door gently behind her. As she climbed into her silver two door sporty car, and started the engine, she thought about how it would be completely out of place somewhere like Wyoming. She would need to get a four wheeled drive SUV. Well, there was plenty of money for that.

She wasn't going to get dinner though. She had some-where else to be first.

CHAPTER 52

"I need to speak with Sheriff Carter. It's very important."

Doris peered over her wire rimmed glasses at the woman. She remembered Elena Rivera. It hadn't been an hour since they left. *She is too pretty for her own good*, Doris thought.

"What is this in regards to?" Doris asked.

"It's in regards to the murders of Tommy and Rosie Allen. The same thing we've been coming in here about, you know that. Please, it's imperative that I speak with him right now."

Doris glanced over her shoulder. "He's on the phone. If you will just have a seat, I'll see that he gets the message as soon as he is off."

"No."

Doris raised her eyebrows. "No?"

"That's right. No. This can't wait."

"Well, it will have to…"

Doris stopped speaking midway through as she watched Elena blow past her and made a beeline to the sheriff's office.

"Ma'am, please you can't go in there!"

The words were lost to the walls as Elena was almost to

the sheriff's office door before Doris could peel her large frame from her chair and start after her.

Elena could see the sheriff was still on the phone, but she didn't care. She opened his office door and walked in. "I need to speak to you."

Sheriff Carter took one look at her. He could see the distress on her face. "Um, sir, I'll call you back." He hung up the phone before the person on the other end had the chance to respond.

Doris poked her head in. "Sorry Jimmy. She got away from me."

He waved her away with a flick of his hand. "It's all right Doris. I'll deal with this."

Doris turned and headed back to her perch at the front desk.

"Mrs. Rivera, I was just on the phone with the D.A., talking about your case. It's rude to interrupt the D.A."

"I'm sorry, but this really can't wait."

"All right, what can I do for you?" He pointed at the chair in front of his desk.

Elena looked at it. "I'd rather stand, thank you."

"Okay, then. Please tell me what is going on."

"My husband killed Tommy and Rosie."

"I know."

Her eyes went wide. "You do?"

"Yeah. Like I said earlier, we are pretty sure he killed them. We are still working on proving it though, since he didn't admit to that. How do you know he did it? Were you there?"

"No, I wasn't there. But he told me he did."

"Okay, let's talk. Would you like to sit now, so we can have a conversation?" He indicated the chair once again.

"Okay sure, I'll sit." She took a seat.

"Anything to drink? Water, soda, coffee?"

"Nah, I'm good, thanks."

"All right then. Tell me exactly what your husband told you."

Elena told the sheriff everything that Sergio had told her, in great detail. She didn't want to leave anything out. She told him everything that had happened on the night of the home invasion, including the fact that she really did shoot Angelo and Dante. She felt that he would be more likely to believe her, if she got it all out.

Other than the money. She never said a word about the money.

The sheriff told her that he had spoken at great length with the District Attorney. The D.A. had already told him that they would probably not be pressing charges against her for the self-defense shootings. They had found a woman's DNA on Dante's clothing and body, even after having been buried for several months. It was pretty clear what had gone on there that night, and he believed her.

"We also have other evidence. We found the remnants of a matchbook, that we are working on linking back to Sergio. And the gas cans he used. At least one of them didn't entirely melt in the fire. There were no usable fingerprints, but there is gas station video of him filling a couple of gas cans right around the time of the fire. So yeah, we got him."

Without him having to even ask, Elena offered her DNA.

An hour later, all hell broke loose.

CHAPTER 53

Sheriff Carter, Deputy Jones, and three more deputies from the local police department knocked on the front door belonging to the Riveras. Sergio's eyes went wide when he saw who it was.

He opened the front door. Five guns pointed squarely at his chest.

"What is going on here?" he asked.

"Put your hands up in the air!" Sheriff Carter demanded.

"Why? I don't understand what this is all about."

"Do what I said. Right now."

"Yeah, yeah, okay." His arms went up.

"I need to speak to my wife, but she isn't here right now. She can clear this up. Can you just talk to her?"

"I don't think so. Now turn around and put your hands behind your back." All five guns hadn't budged.

Sergio did as he was told. Deputy Jones put on the hand-cuffs and began leading him to his car.

That's when Sergio spotted her. She was standing behind one of the sheriff's cars and watching him.

"Elena! What is going on? Call my attorney," he called to her.

Elena didn't move. It took a moment before realization hit him. *Oh my god. She did it. She told them everything.*

"You?" The hurt on his face was evident. "You did this? You told them? Why would you do that? We had a plan. I loved you."

Elena didn't respond.

"You bitch! I'll never forgive you for this. When I get out of this, I'm gonna kill you!"

"Shut up." Deputy Jones opened the car door and directed Sergio in, head first. He was still screaming at his wife.

Sheriff Carter walked over and joined her. "Don't pay him any mind. After killing your friends, he's not getting out, probably ever."

She nodded. "Yeah, I know. But the problem is that he has the type of friends who will kill for him. Like those two men you found. I mean, he told them to kill Tommy and Rosie, just for some gold and jewelry they had hidden at their cabin, and they had every intention of doing just that. He had no idea things would go sideways though. I'm just terrified that he'll figure out a way to get someone to come after me. Even from prison, you know?"

"Yeah, I know," Sheriff Carter told her. "Maybe you should find somewhere to start over."

"Yeah, I think that's a great idea."

CHAPTER 54

FOUR AND A HALF YEARS LATER

"Mommy, mommy! I found four eggs! Just like me. I'm four now." The little girl held out the hem of her flowery t-shirt that cradled the eggs.

"Wow, that's awesome. Bring them in. We'll make some breakfast," Elena told her daughter.

After Sergio was arrested, she began to think that a small farm in Wyoming wasn't such a bad idea.

The first thing she did back home was head for the woods. Sergio had been kind enough to tell her exactly where he had hidden the million dollars he had stolen from their friends on that fateful night. She wanted to be sure to get it before he told someone else where to find it. They might stash it for him. Or, more likely, keep it for themselves.

On a brisk spring day, Elena drove the long dirt road to

the abandoned campsite next to the lake. She sat at the long forgotten picnic table next to the water for a little while, just reflecting on everything that had happened. She also wanted to make sure she was completely alone. If anyone was nearby, it could be perilous for them to find her digging next to the rock. They would certainly be curious and might decide that a duffle bag full of money was worth more than her life.

She caressed her still flat belly as she watched the ducks gliding along the glassy lake surface. Sergio would be thrilled to know that he was about to be a father. But that would never come to be. Elena had no intention of him ever finding out. She was terrified that he could still get to her, even from prison.

Eventually, she got up, fetched the shovel from the trunk of her car and made her way to the giant cedar tree that they had dubbed "our spot."

She stood under it, remembering the good times. And they *were* good times. She and Sergio had been deeply in love back then. She had no doubt about that. But after he put their lives at risk by hiring those two thugs, she could never trust him again. She could never truly love him again. He was in essence dead to her.

She would come back for the trial, but that was it. It was several months out and the sheriff assured her it would be after she had given birth. Yes, he knew her little secret. It was one he would take to the grave.

She intended to never set eyes on her husband again. The divorce papers had already been filed. It was only a matter of time before that chapter of her life was over for good.

Walking around behind the tree, she walked over to the boulder and began digging. It didn't take long for her to hit upon the duffle bag. Before pulling it out of the hole, she took another look around for anyone watching. She laughed when she realized she was being ridiculous. Who would be there watching her? If anyone was around, they would be hiking and paying her no mind.

Pulling it out of the ground, she knelt down and unzipped it. A quick glance told her that all, or at least most of the money was still there. She smiled.

~

It took her only a couple of months to get her house packed up and sold. During that time, she had spent a few thousand dollars on a new birth certificate, ID, and passport for herself. She didn't want to take any chances that Sergio's goons could find her.

As long as she stayed offline, paid cash for everything, and lived a simple life, she felt pretty secure that she, and her child, could live a carefree, happy life in Wyoming.

~

"Okay, sweetheart, scrambled eggs for you?"

"Yummy!"

Elena laughed as she watched her beautiful daughter gently cradle the eggs she had gathered for breakfast. The beautiful oranges and violets of the morning were lighting up the gorgeous Wyoming sky.

~

Have you read the Ivy Mystery Series? It's time travel with a twist.

THE MANY LIVES OF IVY WELLS
by Michelle Files

Ivy Wells never wanted to die. When she does, she thinks it's all over. It isn't.

When the 30 year old mother of two wakes up as a 12 year old, she has to navigate her life all over again. And she remembers everything, including the serial killer who is terrorizing her small town.

Ivy Mystery Series:
  The Many Lives of Ivy Wells - Book 1
  The Many Lives of Sam Wells - Book 2
  The Many Lives of Jack Wells - Book 3
  The Many Lives of Georgie Wells - Book 4

Author Note

Thank you for reading my book. As an author, your support is extremely important. If you liked this book, please leave a great review on the site you purchased it from. And please consider reading one of my other titles. :-)

~

If you enjoyed this book and would like information on new releases, sign up for my newsletter here:

www.MichelleFiles.com
Thank you!